Alice Morris

Dragons and cherry blossoms

Alice Morris

Dragons and cherry blossoms

ISBN/EAN: 9783337270919

Printed in Europe, USA, Canada, Australia, Japan

Cover: Foto ©Andreas Hilbeck / pixelio.de

More available books at **www.hansebooks.com**

DRAGONS
AND
CHERRY
BLOSSOMS

By

Mrs. Robert
C. Morris...

New York
Dodd, Mead
& Company
1896

TO

MY HUSBAND.

Clad in native costume

MANY have been before me, and the theme of this volume can hardly be called new, for Japan has been viewed from every side and through all kinds of eyes. This, however, has not deterred me from jotting down a few observations and experiences of my own, hoping that in them my readers may feel some rays of the Orient sunshine and beauty.

I desire to thank Mr. Burton J. Hendrick for the kind and sympathetic aid given upon the manuscript.

CONTENTS.

FOREIGN RESIDENTS.

FOREIGN RESIDENTS.

YOUR visit to Japan is likely to be a succession of surprises. Our discovery of the country is so recent that the large amount of literature on the subject frequently fails to change your childhood impression of that distant land. European travellers often entertain us with their ideas of America as an uncultivated waste with an occasional hastily constructed town, in which the red man is still to be seen; and my notions of the land of the Mikado were somewhat similar. I could never think of the Orient without thinking of the mushroom hat; and for me Japan meant a succession of bamboo huts, almond-eyed men with long and low-hanging moustaches, an occasional china cup, and now and then a strangely decorated fan. I was not at all sure that it was a hospitable shore to visit; I understood that heads were removed there upon the slightest provocation. My earliest knowledge was gained from the paper lanterns that were the delight of Fourth-of-July celebrations,

and those remarkably adorned napkins familiar to patrons of church fairs. I was also frequently called upon to make Sunday-School contributions

16

for the conversion of these abandoned souls, and have vivid recollections of listening to many addresses by daring spirits, who had actually returned from the dangerous soil. After such occasions as these, I always looked upon the principal occupation of the Japanese as the stoning of missionaries. As I grew older, I tried to educate myself into different ideas, but all the books that I read, and even an occasional Japanese friend that I made, did not succeed in doing away with my childish fancies.

And so, when I found myself sailing into the Port of Yokohama one bright April morning, the ideal Japan of years gone by was what was uppermost in my mind. At first I thought there must be some mistake, for there was nothing to be seen in this harbour to correspond with the strange delights of my dreams. Not a single one-storied, thatched house, such as used to grace the pages of my geography, was visible on the shore. Everything, as far as I could see, was the same as the entrance to an European seaport. The long array of wharves might perhaps be missing, but there was many a ship built on western lines, and occasionally a small steam-tug went puffing by, the whistle blowing as naturally as in any western harbour. And, even as I looked beyond all this, towards the shore, there was no visible sign that I had reached Japan. "Those people who make pictures of Japanese life do not tell the truth," I thought to myself, completely bewildered. When I landed, I found large brick houses of a most occidental kind, and shops fitted out in the regular English style. Not only were the outward evidences of life most un-Japanese, but few of the people passing up and down the street had the almond eyes, the short, wiry hair, or the olive complexion that I had quitted America to see ; and young nurse girls wheeled about little carriages containing the same kind of babies that I had left three thousand miles away. Children in little trim English clothes, with their little English bare legs, were walking about and occasionally disappearing behind English hedges into houses of a distinctly Queen Anne type.

While I was surveying all this with a startled air, I was delighted and relieved by the sight of several small Orientals who ran quickly up to the wharf, dragging behind them peculiar two-wheeled conveyances. Yes, after all, here was some indication of the thing for which I had been looking ; these were men of Japan, it was true, but hardly the Japanese of whom I had dreamed. They seemed rather out of place in this European city, and did not assume an aggressive air at all, as they politely offered to carry us to the hotel in their strange vehicles.

The explanation of this state of affairs is, however, very satisfactory. When you reach Yokohama, you land at what is called the Settlement, which is the portion of the city set aside by the Government for the foreign residents. Japan itself is situated back of this, and there, if you jump again into your *jinrikisha* and take another ride, you will find that it is Japan indeed.

There is one great hotel at Yokohama, — a genuine European importation, with large parlours, reading and sitting rooms, electric lights and bells. Your *jinrikisha* man immediately takes it for granted that you wish to stop

at the Grand Hotel, and without waiting for instructions, hurries you off
to Ni-jiu-ban, as it is called in the
vernacular. You will probably arrive
during the season of travel, and so be
enabled to see the house at its best.
If one or two of the foreign ships are
in the harbour, and the officers come
ashore, a scene of unusual attractiveness is sure to follow. A military
band plays during dinner, commonly
discoursing the patriotic airs of the
different nations, though a well-known
western march is frequently inter-
spersed. The rooms are trimmed
with flowers; there are ladies in
bright, pretty gowns, men in evening
dress, and Japanese "boys" in blue
tights, white coats, and stocking feet.
The gathering is decidedly cosmopolitan. You can talk with an American
on stocks, an Englishman on golf, a
Frenchman on Panama, or a Russian

on the Triple Alliance. If you only step out on the piazza and take a short stroll, you will have a fine opportunity to gratify your taste for contrast, for it will be stepping from the Occident to the Orient. Perhaps the moon is shining — and the moon seems to shine differently in Japan than at home. There, below you, lies the land you thought you were being cheated out of; there are the small one-storied houses, the narrow streets, all bathed in the silence that so well fits your mood. A few lights are blinking below, but for the most part you see only what the moonlight cares to reveal. Off in the harbour are large shadowy forms which you know are western vessels, and your spirit feels a touch of old-fashioned patriotism at the thought that one of them is flying the American flag. The sound of the music comes from the

distance, and you know that the dancing has begun; but you care little at
the present time for such occidental
diversions.

In the morning the sun will probably be shining in a truly oriental way,

and you think it might be well to take
a drive. Probably the first thing you
will see, will be a large number of
young Japanese girls, apparently out

for a walk. Though they are clad in their own native costumes and have a general appearance that is decidedly Japanese, there is yet an air about them suggestive of the West. You puzzle over the matter for some time, and at last, with a sudden burst of intelligence, exclaim: "A boarding-school." And you are right; these young girls are being trained in the usages of the best English society, and have begun to dabble in French and algebra in a true boarding-school style. As they pass you by and you go on, you will see many small children attended by Japanese *amahs*, and baby carriages meet you everywhere. There are also a few shops scattered around, and looking to the left you will see the British flag waving above the marine hospital. A little further on, your heart gives a bound, for you see the stars and stripes waving in the breeze, and you think that being an American is not so bad after all, whatever the foreigner may say of our confusion of "baggage" and "luggage" and our use of ice-water at dinner. It is the American hospital, a large, old-fashioned building, comfortable and home-like, with a garden filled with flowers and tropical plants. You can look from here into the bay, and the ship so dimly perceived the night before, you see is the "Baltimore." You keep in the road, pass more Queen Anne houses and pretty green hedges, and an occasional bungalow ; and further on you meet a park that has been laid out by the foreigners. Here are more baby carriages and bare legged children, and several prettily arranged tennis courts in which the players are enjoying themselves in a genuine English way.

It is probably a holiday, and the

people will soon turn out for a cele-
bration. It is hard to find a day in
Japan that is not a holiday. It is well
to know this before you visit the
country, or you will be very much
inconvenienced. You will be likely
to visit the bank, and be much surprised to find it closed. "Why?"
you will ask a friend, and he will
answer: "It is a holiday." And
what is the day celebrated? Perhaps
the fall of the Bastile; perhaps the
discovery of the Gunpowder Plot;
perhaps Washington's birthday, the
Fourth of July, or one of the innumerable sacred days of the Japanese. The
trouble is that there are so many different nationalities in Japan, each
demanding that certain events be
respectfully observed, that only on
about one-third of the calendar days
can business be transacted. It is a
country of a perennial holiday. There

are a great many ways in which
properly to observe these occasions,
and a large number of entertainments
are arranged. If you wish, you can
attend the theatre, — not the an-
ciently-established institution of the
country, but a genuine play, such as
you sometimes see in the Occident.
I qualify the statement because I think
it seldom that you will permit yourself to attend such execrable performances at home as draw crowded
houses of intelligent people at Yokohama. They are given by strolling
players on their way around the
world, who stop at the principal Japanese cities and foist their wares upon
a diversion-craving public. They entertain you with the misfortune of
the " Forsaken Leah," the mistakes
and unavailing repentance of " Bob
Briley," the " Ticket-of-leave-man,"
or you may have the opportunity of

weeping through five acts of "East Lynne," or "The Elopement." A minstrel show has been known to come ashore, and an exhibition of French marionettes is no uncommon sight.

Perhaps your nature requires a different kind of excitement ; if so, you may attend the races. These are carried on in the true English style, and are very generously patronised. The occasions are holidays in themselves, and offer a sufficient excuse for the closing of the banks and stores. A race track has been laid out back of the residence portion of the city, and has an additional attractiveness in the fact that it commands an excellent view of the elusive Fuji. Foreigners turn out in full force, many coming down from Tokio. Often the Mikado honours the affair with his presence ; he is always an interesting addition to any event, but he is an inconvenient person to have around, owing to a peculiar phase of Japanese veneration. No one may hold his head higher than the Mikado, else his sacredness would be outraged; and the many attempts to make him tower above the rest of the populace frequently produce amusing complications. Such a predicament happened a short time ago, when the Mikado was on his way to the races. An American with more curiosity than knowledge of Japanese religious rites, thought it a fine opportunity to catch a glimpse of the royal person, and so elevated himself upon a box near by and awaited the procession. He had stood there some time, flattering himself upon the difference between American and Oriental intelligence, when his peace of mind was suddenly disturbed by a series of shouts, which, he divined from the gesticulations, were directed towards himself. The constant motions to descend he regarded with a true Yankee stoicism, and it was not until the box was pulled from beneath his feet, that he was induced to pay the proper respect to the Majesty of Japan. The races themselves, with the little shaggy horses, have proved to be a very fertile means of entertainment. The riding is done to a considerable extent by the little Japs, who take to it quite readily, and make very acceptable jockeys.

One of the most delightful events in the social life of the foreign residents of Yokohama is Regatta Day. All their pent-up enthusiasm seems to let itself out, and the numerous visiting vessels contribute to a most entertaining scene. The contests take place in the spring, and preparations are made many days in advance. The

"The dainty *kimono*-clad forms."

vessels in the harbour are gayly decorated with flags and streamers ; the
wealthier classes turn out in their carriages, and the Bund is one mass of
ladies and children in white dresses,
intermingled by the dainty *kimono*-
clad form of the Japanese. The hotel
is impartially adorned with the colours
of every nation, and the piazza is a
varied scene of moving gayety. Every
one does not attend the races behind
the bluff, but Regatta Day is the one
event of the season, and furnishes an
excuse for considerably more than the
nautical contests. The races themselves are perhaps not of sufficient
importance to justify all this excitement, but Yokohama is very different from New York harbour. The day
is bound to be clear, the sky is always
of Italian deepness, and the sun never
fails to shine down on the lively scene
with a refreshing glow.

3   33

Domestic life in Japan has its inconveniences; but it has also its more advantageous side. Do you wish to live in splendid style on a small income? You should dwell in the land where servants cost only four dollars a month. The life of the foreign residents in Japan is somewhat mysterious; the position of the mistress of the household eluded my investigations for a long time. " What do you do? " was a question I asked many of the ladies, but never received a satisfactory reply. After much thought I have come to the conclusion that the only thing your position requires of you is to sit in your parlour and amuse yourself as best you may; and when you wish anything done, simply clap your hands and cry " Boy."

This last word is the keynote to the situation. As soon as you have learned the word "Boy," you have solved the whole problem of the European household in Japan. Everything centres around this important dignitary, whom even foreign innovation has not succeeded in abolishing. The "Boy" has edged his way into every foreign home in Japan, and his position is as firmly established as the homes themselves. He is one of the most indispensable domestic functionaries that have figured in history. But, in the first place, an excusable mistake must be corrected. The "Boy" is not a boy at all, but is simply called so in deference to custom. Most of the "Boys" have large families of their own, and I have seen many with white hair and wrinkled faces. He never seems to resent this youthful title, and would feel very much bewildered should you suddenly begin to call him "Man."

He appreciates his important position very keenly ; he is no ordinary servant, but a man with thoughts of his own and the dignity of a household resting upon his shoulders.

The whole thing is managed somewhat after this style : You receive an intimation that a few friends will dine with you, and this intimation is all about which you need trouble yourself. You never begin to think what you have to offer your guests, for you are not supposed to know anything about such things. You simply sit down, clap your hands and shout " Boy ! " In a few moments the door will open and the person who bears this title presents himself. He approaches, bows lowly, and makes a single ejaculation, —

" Heh ! "

This simply means that he is all attention. If you are inexperienced, you will get the idea that this word means "yes." But you will have many opportunities later to correct your mistake. The Japanese says "Heh!" to signify that he is listening, and there his responsibility ends. He never commits himself.

"I am going to have two friends to dinner," you reply, and you give their names.

"Heh!"

He bows again, turns around, and leaves the room. That is all you have to do until the dinner hour arrives. Never make any suggestions; the "Boy" would be completely mystified by such a proceeding. The way he goes about everything is very picturesque. You understand that the man who has just made his exit is the head "Boy" or No. 1 "Boy." He goes downstairs and begins to examine the possibilities for the dinner.

Very likely he finds something lacking. If so, he immediately makes a
call on No. 1 " Boy " next door, and
returns with the supplementary dish
needed to make the dinner a success.
There exists a kind of free-masonry
among the " Boys," and what one
cannot find in his own domain he
feels no hesitation in borrowing from
a friend near by. Your " Boy " then
visits the " Boys " of the friends who
are to dine with you and makes many
interesting inquiries. He asks what
their favourite wines are, and never
hesitates to request a loan of their
plate and linen. He usually also demands the cooks of your friends, and
leads them off to your house in order
that the dinner may be more satisfac-
torily prepared. Thus it happens
that when your friends arrive they are
very likely to eat your dinner cooked
by their own servants and to see their

own china and linen gracing your table. More than this, the " Boys " of your friends are usually present and attend to their wants. The order of things will be reversed when you dine out.

You see this " Boy " is a very convenient and important person, and as he is usually an intelligent man, everything goes smoothly on. Occasionally a difficulty arises owing to the fact that he has not a sufficient regard for the mistress of the house, and indeed it is a question whether he ever looks upon her as such. Japan has not yet learned to rate women at their true worth, and it is this sentiment that is at the bottom of the " Boy's " reluctance to take orders from anyone but a man. Most of them are gradually coming around and will obey you, but a few conservative souls still remain. I had a friend who

possessed a very worthy " Boy,"
whose character was blemished by
this one defect. She told him one
day to remove a plant into an adjoining room. He bowed, said " Heh !"
and departed. Some hours passed,
and the plant was still unmoved. He
was called in again, again he bowed,
ejaculated the usual " Heh !" and left
the room. My friend tried this
several times, and succeeded in getting
more bows and more " Hehs !" but
the plant remained where it had been.
She spoke to her husband about the
matter, who called in the " Boy " and
told him to remove the object of the
dispute. The " Boy " bowed, said
" Heh !" took the plant and carried it
into an adjoining room. When asked
to explain his previous disobedience,
he said : " I will do it if master wishes
it, heh !" and with a profound obei-
sance he retired.

Another great enemy to domestic life is what is known as the " Squeeze." This is not peculiar to the household, but is found in every part of the Japanese social system. The whole business of the country is run on a commission. Every time you buy anything, you have to pay several "squeezes," or commissions, to the various people concerned in the transaction. No " Boy" will run an errand without his " squeeze," and he uses a great deal of liberty in your domestic accounts. Should you send him out to buy a bouquet of flowers, he would always charge you as well as the florist a " squeeze" in the reckoning. The butcher who deals with you has to pay him a certain amount, and of course you are the one who suffers in the end. This is altogether independent of the profit of the goods, and often is little more than a personal consideration. Foreigners have made war many times against the "squeeze," but their efforts have been unsuccessful. It seems to be a second nature with the Japanese; it is one of those good old customs that they will not let die. I had an iconoclastic friend who resolved that there should be no "squeezes" to impede her domestic calculations, and who decided upon a reform. She thought that she would begin modestly at first, and hit upon the lamps to experiment on. There is a very humble person whose occupation it is to go from door to door and fill all the lamps of his customers, but his pay is not too small to necessitate a little "squeeze" to the head "Boy" for the privilege. The lady in question decided to hire this boy directly, and for a time she thought the plan was succeeding remarkably well. One day, however, she found that her head "Boy" had a pleasing custom of making a round of the lamps every morning and removing a certain quantity of the oil. By selling what he procured this way, he recovered the " squeeze" of which he had been defrauded.

The specialising tendency of the people is another thing particularly irritating to those who live in Japan. Such a thing as a man-of-all-work who goes around picking up odd jobs is an unknown phenomenon. You must have a large number of servants or you will get nothing done. A certain "Boy" puts the coal in the stove and another cooks the dinner. But the "Boy" who does the cooking would never touch the coal, if you had a dozen guests waiting upstairs. It is a matter of caste, and one occupation is immeasurably superior to another; at least, in the opinion

43

of him who practises it. You have a " Boy " who takes care of the horses, but he would not understand you at all should you ask him to drive them. If a light needs turning up, and you request your head " Boy " to do it, he would never think of obeying. He would rather run two blocks to fetch the menial whose duties are along that line. I was told a story of a lady on shipboard, who requested her attending " Boy " to close an open port-hole. He answered " Heh ! " and went out to search for the servant who attended to such matters. It took him fifteen minutes to find him, but he finally led him triumphantly in, and the port-hole was closed. It had never occurred to the former that he ought to do it himself ; he had not been educated to that position in society, and it would have grated harshly against his sense of the fitness of things to suggest that he was fully qualified to close port-holes. Every Japanese has a great pride in his task, knows his own place, and thinks that the greatest requirement of a virtuous life is that he does not interfere with the duties of others.

SHOPPING.

SHOPPING.

YOU will have many friends who will give you a great deal of kindly advice before you leave for Japan. On no point will their suggestions be as plentiful as on the mooted question of shopping. With a knowledge born of experience, they will inform you that these almond-eyed Orientals are not the guileless souls that they may seem, and that

beneath all their gentleness of manners there lies a keen wit which
will tax your American sharpness to
the utmost. They may perhaps go
further and descend to particulars,
and you will have the opportunity of
learning the number of tricks you
will be subjected to and the large
amount of wares that are being reserved until you land. All this advice
you will carefully note, and think that
when you start down the streets of
Tokio or Yokohama you have an advantage over your compatriots, and
that you are secure from the dangers
of early shopping in a new country.
You have all the words of your friend
in mind, and decide to wait several
days before you make a single purchase. At about this point of your
self-congratulations you will catch
sight of a small two-story building,
and for some inconceivable reason be

attracted within. Perhaps it is the
dainty sign over the door; perhaps
the smiling face of the host, who
looks upon you with so inviting an
air; perhaps the ever-attendant evil
spirit of shopping that has begun to
work his baneful spell. At any rate,
in a short time you find yourself in
a small room surrounded by a delightful collection of
bric-à-brac, with
a cup of tea in
your hand and
the happy face
of the proprietor
beaming down
upon you. An
hour or two slips by, and when you
leave you will suddenly discover that
you have ordered a large part of the
merchant's wares, and that you have a
neat little bill smilingly presented to
you. It is not until you are in the

street again, or perhaps easefully reposing in your room at the hotel, that the whole terrible truth flashes upon you. You have done just what you were told not to do, and just what you had considered yourself firmly guarded against. A horrible suspicion crosses your mind. What if all those charming things you bought belonged to the worthless class your friend had so conscientiously warned you of; and what if the genial smile of the merchant were but the mask of a deceiving heart? In a day or two your suspicion will have been confirmed. The goods that you so rashly purchased will be given as a present to your attending "Boy," and your shopping henceforth will become rather a scientific than an emotional affair.

The Japanese are rapidly learning the proper use to be made of tourists,

and are always ready to receive them.
You will not have been long in your
room when a gentle knock will be
heard at the door, and a most obsequious Oriental will make his entrance. He will bow with the utmost
profoundness, and present you with
a card which contains his name and
crest, — usually in the form of a
teacup or fan. You return his gaze as
kindly as possible. He says: " Please
you come see my shop," makes another
bow, and retires. The whole scene is
not unpleasing to you, and you are
thinking it over as an interesting
experience when another knock is
heard. Another Jap of the same appearance as your former visitor now
enters, makes a similar bow, gives
you his card, says : " Please you come
see my shop," and as gracefully takes
his leave. If you are wise you will
now determine to receive no more

callers, for this sort of thing will be kept up all day, and you will have a varied assortment of cards before the evening comes. Your new friends are most scrupulously polite and have no air of bluster or eagerness; but they are quietly persistent, and would not think of passing you by without giving you a chance to learn of the advantages of their house. They keep a careful watch for the arrival of every new steamer, and trace all the passengers to the different hotels. The reputation of the American as the generous spender of millions is as firmly fixed in the minds of the Japanese as in those of less distant lands, and to them they give a large amount of attention.

Indeed, it is generally assumed by everyone you meet that you have come to Japan to shop, and the kindest favour he can do you is to

show you how and where you can
do so with the best results. Even
the humble coolie, who carries you
around in your *jinrikisha*, firmly be-
lieves this, and thinks that if he is in
a small measure the means of your
making a happy purchase, his way
into your affections is won. If you
tell him in the morning that you wish
to take a ride, he will tuck you comfortably in and start at a rapid pace
towards the main thoroughfare of the
city. You will be quietly enjoying
everything you see, and will, perhaps,
be somewhat surprised when the
coolie suddenly stops before one of
those two-story buildings with which
you are now so familiar, and glances
up into your face with the most self-
congratulating expression. If you do
not immediately descend and enter
the shop, he will suddenly become
crestfallen, and wear a look that

55

means that you are quite unable to appreciate a favour, and do not know a good thing when you see it. The chances are, however, that you will feel an invisible force attracting you within the little shop, and so leave your coolie without, a happy man.

If you are in Japan during a period of silver depression, you are a very unfortunate person indeed. You have perhaps visited the bank the day before and changed a thousand dollars of your gold into two thousand dollars of silver, and this unexpected increase in your worldly possessions is the very worst thing that could have happened to you. For you are likely to get the idea that you can now afford to be a little extravagant; that you have just twice as much money as you had before, and that you would be a very stingy person, did you not scatter a little of it about. You have probably, however, one advantage in the fact that you have shopped before, and do not think that there is much danger that the experience of a few days ago will be repeated. By this time your respect for your anxious friend, who so vainly gave you his advice, has greatly increased ; and you decide that when you return you will make a point of breathing the same gentle counsel in the ears of all you meet who are on their way to the land of the cherry-blossom and the almond-eyed sharper.

The street in which most of the shops are found has the delicious local flavour that seldom fails to entice the unwary purchaser. The thoroughfare is very narrow, and is lined by two rows of shed-like buildings adorned in front by hanging cloth signs. Many of these signs are inscribed with the name of the keeper, who does not confine himself to the Japanese characters, but frequently spells himself out in English, —a thing that you are likely to take as a personal compliment to yourself. The cloths are also sometimes covered with emblematic figures representative of the goods sold within. There are grotesque and unheard of birds; armour, and paintings representing the god of money and good luck. The lower story of the house is probably open to the street, but it is sometimes hidden by a curtain of blue and white, which an attendant lifts to allow you to enter. Really, there is nothing in all this that tells you of the treasures that lie beyond, but you have a sensation which for the time being seems uncontrollable. Sometimes, on a holiday, the whole scene may be changed, and by the addition of a large number of paper lanterns and clusters of wistaria and cherry-blossoms an element of festivity is introduced. But the grotesque methods of advertising that you are familiar with as an American, are unknown to the Japanese, and utterly distasteful to their sense of propriety. Even in the marking of prices they exercise the greatest taste, using little thin strips of cloth with the cost of the article painted in blue. This, however, you do not see until you enter the shop. The proprietor will receive you with the utmost politeness, but there is no sign of unpleasant aggressiveness in his behaviour. He views your visit both from a social and business point of view, and esteems your notice of him as a personal favour. Even though you do not buy, he always takes pleasure in showing what he has to sell. He likes to have you show some appreciation of his goods; and if you have done this, you can leave without buying a thing and be sure of as warm a welcome when you return. One demand he will make of you, and that is, that you take plenty of time. He likes to talk and discuss, and seems dissatisfied unless you consider the transaction as one of great importance and worthy of much meditation. The hurried visits that he sometimes receives from Americans, who rush in and wish to do everything in a few moments, utterly bewilder him. He is willing to spend a whole day with a single customer, and never shows any impatience except when you are in a hurry. He greets you with a profound bow, and smilingly places his shop at your disposal. He usually has one or two assistants who keep at a respectful distance until their services are re-

quired. The host is very quiet, and
does not begin to praise everything
in the room, but calmly calls your

attention to each article, and relies
upon your own good taste to see its
virtues. His first floor is usually
given up to a large display of ancient

armour and swords, each piece with a history of its own, and speaking terrible tales of the good old fighting days of the Shoguns. There are grotesque and grinning masks that the most stoical temperament cannot gaze at without shuddering, and frequent representations of the Japanese conception of the Devil that make you suddenly turn your back and become interested in something of a less religious aspect. The weapons are what delight many a warlike spirit; Japan has always been famous for its steel, and many of these swords might make one think that the days of the famous blades of old had returned. All these are now, of course, as antique to the Japanese as to ourselves, for their usefulness, except as interesting curios, has been replaced by the more prosaic implements of modern warfare.

If you are a woman you will not be likely to buy any of these articles of war, and you will find it a relief to escape the fiery eyes and low-hanging tongue of that mask in the corner. The proprietor calls your attention to a rickety staircase, and invites you to ascend into the second story. By so doing, you will soon find yourself in a little room which reveals altogether a different sight to the one below. You have left the domain of war and blood, and are now surrounded by suggestions of religion and art. There are Buddhas of every kind, — wooden, bronze, and gold; there are dainty little teapots, porcelains, candlesticks, and altar-pieces, to satisfy the most exacting taste; there are highly-polished mirrors gracing the walls, and another collection of swords, of a perhaps less warlike appearance than those below.

The scene has graceful touches, for the small children of the family are huddled together on the floor, amusing themselves with such Japanese playthings as grasshoppers and crickets. These are their dolls, and they would never lay them aside for the less animated toys of the Western world. The wife of the proprietor is always at hand, who supplements the bows of her husband with dimpled smiles of her own, and who treats you with a respect that is not too distant to be friendly. She is sitting on the floor in front of a small *bibachi*. You have not been in the room long before you hear that little quiet steaming that you now know so well, and soon the little woman rises and, with a smile and bow, leaves the room.

All this is very delightful, and it requires all your presence of mind

"The wife of the Proprietor."

and the recollections of a previous day's experience to keep you from falling into a snare. You know very well that all these dazzling things about you have more glitter than gold, and that they are manufactured expressly for unknowing foreigners, such as you are assumed to be. You may be sure, that there are finer goods than these, kept carefully out of sight. The merchants never display their choicest wares on the shelves, but have them neatly tied up in boxes in an adjoining room. In some way you hint to your suave friend that you have shopped before, and are perfectly familiar with the peculiar tricks of the trade. All this he receives with an intelligent smile, and asks you to seat yourself. If you look around for a chair you will betray yourself as less experienced than you claim, so you had better drop at once on your heels; for by doing so, you will immediately gain a point in the good graces of your host.

And now a delicate patter is heard on the stairs, and the little woman who left a few moments ago returns. She has a small tray full of cups and sweetmeats, which she deposits on the floor as she sits down in front of you. The proprietor joins the group, and occasionally one or two of the children forego their grasshoppers and crickets, and supply the sole element lacking to a very pretty domestic picture. The tea is now poured out; you are expected to drink several cups, else the shopping that is to follow would not be a success. The host says many pretty things, rejoices at the fact that you are an American, and thinks your country the crowning triumph of modern civilization. He trusts that your health is as good as your rosy cheeks and sparkling eyes would lead one to believe, and that nothing will happen to make your journey in Japan anything but one of the delightful memories of your after-life. Meanwhile you sip the pale drink, nibble at the cakes and candies, think your charming new friend not the crafty schemer you know him to be, and are almost led to believe that you have come not so much on business as for the sake of making a morning call.

But now the host claps his hands, and an attendant appears from a rear room, bearing several neat-appearing boxes in his arms. The goods that you have come to buy are in these little square affairs, but you are almost as much interested in the boxes themselves as in what they contain.

They are daintily made of light wood, and are not disfigured by the clumsy nails or cracks that do not annoy our less æsthetic merchant of the West. When the attendant begins to remove the wares your appreciation of the artistic shop-keeper increases, for everything is daintily wrapped up in cloth of alternate red and yellow sides. Japanese paper is of a much choicer kind than ours, but no self-respecting merchant would ever think of using it to cover his wares. You become very familiar with this yellow cloth before you leave the country, for it is as generally used as our less artistic substitute at home.

Perhaps you know what you want and perhaps you don't, but it will make no difference to the proprietor, who prefers that you take plenty of time. He says very little in praise of what he puts before you, though occasionally he will unaggressively remark on the particular qualities of an unusually charming article of bric-à-brac or roll of silk, or drop a word on the depth of colour and finish of a piece of gold lacquer; nor is he willing to let an occasional piece of Satsuma pass by without calling your attention to its delicate shade and crackle.

This goes on for some time, until your eye alights on something that you must have, and then the most interesting feature of the performance begins; for a Japanese merchant is entirely out of harmony with the one-price system of the West, and would never think of asking the actual amount for which he will really sell his wares. He has his price, it is true, but this is only for those of small experience, and from others he seldom hopes to get more than one-third to one-half of what he asks. Never think, however, that you get the best of him, for there is always a limit below which he will never go. Friends of mine have reached this limit, and their most persistent efforts have never succeeded in making the shopkeeper less firm. They would drop into the shop morning after morning and renew their offer; the merchant would smile, but remain unshaken. If you stay very long in Japan you will become so accustomed to this haggling practice, that you will acquire a habit you will have difficulty in shaking off. When, after I returned home, a dry-goods-store clerk told me that the price of a certain article was fifteen dollars, I could hardly keep from replying, "I'll give you ten."

"How much will you sell me this for?" you inquire at last, perhaps picking up a piece of delicate bric-à-brac, which in your fond imagination you already see gracefully reposing on your library table at home.

The shopkeeper looks at it sharply with his little eyes for some time, then answers with a smile, —

"Sixty *yen*."

Your hands go up in horror. "What?" you frantically exclaim; but the merchant answers you with another smile. Your emotion, however, is as feigned as the shopkeeper's apparent firmness, for you know that it will be an easy matter to make him reduce the price, — the main question being whether your limit will be the same as his. The chances are that he will take just about one-third what he asks, and make a handsome profit then. So, you with the proper spirit decide to take him at an even lower figure and reply, —

"I will give you fifteen."

The dejected air that suddenly spreads over his face is the kind of which a Japanese merchant is alone capable. He gives a great sigh and gazes at you with a look that seems to ask if you were born without a heart. His emotion is so great that he may even rise, walk around the shop, and examine several of his dearly beloved curios that have not been subjected to such outrageous treatment. He will soon return, however, and, with the humblest voice in the world and a sadly withered smile, announce his ultimatum, —

"Will give for thirty *yen*."

You shake your head, push the rare object aside, and rise. You do not intend to go, but you begin to look at a different line of goods. The shopkeeper has not lost his politeness, and he takes the utmost pains in showing a large number of things that he knows you never intend to buy. During all this you and he occasionally cast furtive glances at the object of your disagreement, but neither one for a long time makes any allusion to it. Finally, the moment comes for you to go, but you decide to make one more attempt, which you know will be effectual. Picking up the dainty bronze, you say in an off-hand manner that you will give him twenty *yen*.

He looks at you sadly, and then again at the object in your hands. He casts his eyes at the ceiling, bestows a glance upon his innocent children playing with grasshoppers and crickets, all unaware that they are being defrauded of an inheritance, makes the bow of humiliation, and says with a short gasp, —

"I am resigned."

After he has expressed his emotions in this unvarying phrase, his spirits seem once more to return. He smiles again in his old way, and his bows have the old obsequiousness. He even gives you another cup of tea, and in other ways betrays the secret satisfaction that he feels on having made a very good bargain. He follows you down the stairs to the awaiting *jinrikisha* and bids you farewell with the most touching "*Sayonara*" that you have yet heard. As you slowly ride away, the last thing you see is his bowing form in the door, and you give a sigh at the thought that all this display of friendship is but owing to the fact that you have probably paid twice what you should for the dainty bronze statue that is to adorn your library at home.

OUR DINNER AT KIOTO.

OUR DINNER AT KIOTO.

OF course, it could hardly be expected that our dinner would be Japanese in all its features, but it was not only our embarrassment at our surroundings that prevented it from being so. The appearance of our host himself in side-whiskers was enough to give an un-oriental air to the ceremony, and clearly indicated the peculiar mixture of the East and West of which his character pre-

sents a striking example. For he had
visited extensively in America, where
he had performed high diplomatic
functions and carried back many of
our traits, not the least evident of
which were the whiskers above re-
ferred to. It was also unnecessary
to use an interpreter when talking
with him, as he spoke our language
easily and well. As far as politeness went, however, he was entirely
Japanese. I have an indefinite rec-
ollection of him as an embodiment
of smiles and bows; his manners
were perfect, his voice was of unusual sweetness. He had a keen
mind and kept a watchful eye on us
during the evening, in order that the
strangeness of our situation should
add rather a feeling of pleasantness
than of discomfort.

He was a man far advanced in the
ideas of new Japan, and he had gone

so far as to adopt the European costume.   But this evening he had cast
it aside and appeared in all the splendor of a Japanese host. After we
had travelled under the direction of
a little *musmee* with a lighted candle,
through a long, arched lane, we suddenly found ourselves before a small
house and heard the most un-oriental
of all words: "Good evening."   We
looked up, and there stood our host
between two wicker panels which he
had thrust aside, with his handsome
face smiling the most cordial of wel-
comes.   He wore the conventional
divided skirt, and over this a *kimono*
of dark grey, caught together in front
with a cord. His foot-gear was the
customary sandals, which, however,
he did not wear during the evening.
Of course he did not have his wife
with him, for even his progressive
spirit had not reached the point where

he could allow any feminine supervision of his feast. The hostess is unknown in Japan, where domesticity does not play the part it should. We had another proof of this in the invitations we received, which did not invite us to our host's house, but to one of the swell restaurants of Kioto. For a Japanese to entertain at his own house would be a social barbarism.

The length of the Major — one of our party — was often inconvenient in Japan, and I saw him casting troubled glances at the house before which we found ourselves. It was very small, and when we finally entered he found it necessary to stoop in order to get in at all. We did not gain an entrance immediately, for we found an obstacle in our way in the form of the little *musmee* who had conducted us thither. Before starting, the two ladies of the party had debated for a long time what foot-gear they should wear, being faced by the American extreme of shoes and the Japanese extreme of stocking feet. They congratulated themselves that they had hit upon a happy solution, by wearing their party slippers; but when they arrived they found that they had miscalculated. As they stepped upon the platform and were about to enter the room, the little *musmee's* hands went up in horror. We can only appreciate her feelings by imagining our own, should one of our callers elevate his feet upon the parlor furniture. Should they desecrate her

85

spotless white mats with their barbarous American slippers? Our poor host had his hands full, trying to pacify the little enraged body, and at the same time to act towards us as though this outburst was one of the regularly-planned features of the dinner. His ever present smiles were still more in requisition, and he could not bow enough in his endeavour to make us feel at ease. Suddenly, there came a calm; the little maid withdrew, and we were bidden in a most polite way to enter. The offended girl, however, sulked away like an angry child, and I am convinced that if we made any enemies in our trips in Japan, the little *musmee* at this restaurant was one of them.

This was the first Japanese house I had ever been in, and naturally I was interested to see what it was like. It was oriental in every way, though by no means an example of oriental splendor. At one end there was a platform on which incense was burning, and the walls were entirely bare but for two paper *kakemonos*. The floor was covered with white matting, on which were placed black velvet cushions. These were our seats for the dinner, and each of us was supplied, in addition, with a black lacquered candlestick. For some time we stood there waiting for the host to begin, but as we afterwards learned, it is customary at Japanese social functions for that dignitary to follow. He smilingly requested us to be seated as quietly as though he was bidding us to four hours in Paradise, and not to the physical discomfort — almost torture — that it proved to be. The ladies seated themselves with little trouble, but things did not go so well with the poor Major. His legs formed a large part of a body that measured considerably over six feet, and as those six feet had to be disposed of picturesquely in a sitting posture, you will see that we had almost a tragedy on hand. The Major made several spasmodic attempts, and finally threw himself down in a lifeless heap in a way that furnished our host new cause for smiles and bows.

For all this the scene in which we found ourselves had its romantic side. It was early in the evening of a beautiful night in April, the Japanese June. The wicker panels of the house were thrown open, and the warm air came through, scented with the perfume of the cherry-blossoms and bearing delicate sounds from the garden without. We could see the stars from where we sat, and they had that warm, melting lustre that one sometimes sees at home, but

which
is charac-
teristic of an
oriental night. In
front of the house
was one of those famous
miniature gardens that
embody the dainty Japan-
ese taste. A small, sparkling lake was
bordered by the sacred cherry-trees,
which were in full bloom; a passing
breeze had blown many of the blossoms upon the surface of the water.
The shores were covered with dwarf
trees and a few sprays of pansies. All
of this we could clearly see, for the
moon gleamed down upon the scene
with just enough brightness to render
all distinct without removing any of
the enchantment. From the distance

we could hear the faint tinkling of a waterfall. Even the Major's uncomfortable state of body could not prevent him from catching the poetic flavour of all this. But there was more romance ahead. We all felt a disappointment when our host dropped the oriental manner of salutation and simply bowed profoundly; but now we were soon to have Eastern respect at its fullest. Two *musmees* entered, and, falling on their hands and knees, touched their flower-bedecked heads to the floor. In this respectful attitude they remained before us for some seconds, while we wondered whether the occasion demanded any action on our part, when, suddenly, they rose and presented us with handleless cups full of tea — for every dinner in Japan begins with tea. I looked at the host in despair. "Ah! I will explain," he said, with a laugh, and he did so. This is the way you do it : you place the cup in the palms of both hands, twist the fingers into a supporting position (I do not yet fully understand it), and drink between the thumbs. If you are well-enough bred, you will do this with the utmost ease; but if you are not, you may land the tea in your lap, break the china cup, and be put down as an extremely low person. Of course, the fact that we were foreigners warded off any harsh judgment; and besides, I really believe we all of us did manage somehow to get through the crisis in a way that was not entirely disgraceful.

Japanese æstheticism extends to their dinners, which are extremely graceful affairs. Our host, for example, had divided this dinner into four parts, each typical of a season of the year. In this was a hidden compliment; he intended thus to express his regret that we were unable to spend the whole year in Kioto, and his hopes that this evening's pleasure would offer as good a substitute as possible. And in spite of our uncomfortable attitudes and the strangeness of many of the dishes placed before us, I do not think he was entirely unsuccessful. Not the least pleasant part of the dinner, for example, was that which immediately followed the tea drinking. We had hardly handed the cups back to the *musmees*, when they gave to each of us a beautiful wicker basket filled with flowers, — that, at least, is what we thought they were, until we discovered that they were without smell. In fact, it took us some time to find out that they were not flowers at all, but most exquisite candy imitations. They were more than confectionery — they were true works of art.

But there were other surprises in store for us. As we sat admiring these delicate creations, the doors at the rear suddenly opened, and a living wave of colour came fluttering in. At first we could distinguish nothing but a flock of miniature bats, storks, and other creatures which figure exclusively in Japanese natural history, disporting themselves among dainty representations of purple violets, dandelions, and white and pink cherry-blossoms. After recovering from our first surprise we saw that these were small pieces of embroidery on a background of pale greys and shaded blues, and then we caught sight of waving loops of hair in which were intertwined sprays of flowers and fancy pins. This delicate yet somewhat confused mass drew nearer, and we saw

five little faces painted entirely white
with the exception of clearly-defined
spots of red under the eyes and lips,
that were made particularly small by
a skilful handling of the brush. We
could but ejaculate one word:
"*Geisha!*" These were the famous
dancing girls of Japan, who lead, I
fear, not too happy lives in furnish-
ing much of the enjoyment of Japanese social life. It is only ordinary
people who frequent the theatre in
this country, and it falls upon these
little creatures to furnish the higher
classes a large part of their amusement. They dance, they sing, they
joke, act as waiters, and are generally
expected to supply the element of
gaiety without which no dinner can
be thought complete.

The Japanese do not walk, they
flutter; they do not sit down, they
sink. Each of these delicate bits of

humanity bearing a small lacquered tray sank down before the guest she was to serve. They were continually laughing and chattering among themselves, making naive criticisms of our costumes and of ourselves — for the *geishas* are given a great deal of freedom. They were particularly inquisitive about the ladies' dresses, and even went so far as to ask, through the interpreter, the cost of them. They also were anxious to know whether the Americans made them themselves, and how long it took. These materialistic thoughts changed when they caught sight of the ladies' diamonds, which they romantically imagined to have grown on trees. They made endless remarks about us which we did not understand, and from the interpreter's unwillingness to translate many of their speeches, I am

sure the little fault-finders saw much
in us to criticise.

And now the dinner began in earnest. By our sides we discovered

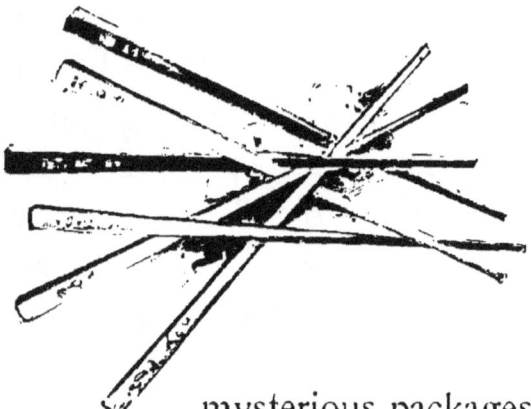

mysterious packages done
up in paper, which we were
horrified to find contained chop-
sticks. This was worse than drinking
tea between your thumbs. It was my
first experience with these utensils,
and I hardly thought myself in a well-
chosen place to learn their mysterious
qualities. I was greatly surprised,
however, to find that it was not so
difficult as it looked, and that chop-

sticks, after all, are not the impossible things the untutored suppose. We had a hard dish to begin on : for after we had got our chop-sticks in battle array, the *geishas* startled us by bringing in soup. More smiles from the host, and more explanations. All you have to do is to eat the solid part with the chop-sticks and drink the liquid as you drink tea. The soup was politely christened "Congratulatory," and was made of green turtle, which is popularly supposed to live a thousand years — another compliment for us. And now that I have begun the menu, I may as well say that the succeeding dishes included fish and eels, and an unprecedented number of soups, cooked *à la Japonaise,* particularly one made of seaweeds, in which their taste was by no means concealed. And there were wines, *homei,* which the Japanese regard as a kind of medicine to prepare the stomach for the food, and *saki*, the national drink, not dissimilar in appearance and taste to a pale, dry sherry.

At this point we were surprised by the arrival of another guest. He had been invited to meet us as a friend of our host, but for some reason had been detained and had sent his excuses. He was clad in the same costume as our host and had also adopted the occidental whiskers, though his were grey. He was not sufficiently Europeanised, however, to omit the Japanese salutation, and consequently prostrated himself " on all fours" before us. He further mystified our minds by presenting each of our party with his card. We looked at our host in despair, who explained that it was customary on such occasions to exchange cards. But we had failed to bring any along, and therefore had to apologise ourselves out of the difficulty as best we could. Of course, our excuses met with the customary smiles.

"We hope you will be able to visit our country sometime," one of us had inspiration enough to say through the interpreter the new arrival had brought with him.

"I have been there already," he replied.

"And how did he like it?"

"It is a very beautiful country, and I hope to go back again sometime."

Though the conversation was satisfactory, the inconvenience always occasioned by the use of an interpreter prevented it from being very lively. The next remark I remember was from the Major, and was not of so suave a kind.

"Say, if I have to sit here much

longer, I shall never be able to use my legs again."

All the evening he had been attempting to gain relief by a constant change of position, but his efforts did not seem to have been successful. We all of us were somewhat tired, but the Major had a great deal more to be tired than we. He had to compose himself, however, for one of the most distinctive features of the dinner.

There was a slight pause after his remark, and we began casting glances at one another and wondering what was to come next. The pause at an American dinner we should consider an awkward one, but our host did not seem to entertain any such idea. Suddenly we heard two snaps that apparently came from stringed instruments, and at the same time the panels in a rear room were

drawn aside. We were taken somewhat by surprise, for we were not
acquainted with the fact that a small
theatrical performance is one of the
usual accompaniments of a Japanese
dinner.

Two of the *geishas* began to play
on the *samisen*, the Japanese banjo,
and the *koto*, a kind of elongated
harp, picked with ivory tips. At

the same time one of the girls came out in the centre of the room, and we had our first sight of Japanese dancing. While she went through the movements of the "Reign of Spring," the two girls with the instruments began singing in that falsetto key which it takes an educated taste to appreciate. They sing so shrilly and the notes they strike are so unnatural, that it becomes a very painful exercise, and will frequently bring tears to the performer's eyes. And how about the dancing? One who is accustomed to the serpentine mazes of our occidental skirt dancers and who likes that sort of thing, may find it hard to enter into the spirit of her Japanese contemporaries; but if you delight in gracefulness in any form, these little *geishas* cannot fail to please. Their costume plays an important part in the series of posturings that makes up the dance, and no small amount of the success achieved depends on the proper manipulation of the fan. You can get the best idea of what it is like, by imagining a succession of dainty tableaux in which the changes are made before your eyes.

After sitting in a Japanese posture on American legs for four hours at a stretch, it was with some difficulty that we finally arose and prepared to leave. As we went out into the night we were followed by a veritable chorus of "*Sayonara*," which is the Japanese word for "good-bye." We were somewhat surprised to be followed by the little *musmees*, bringing as gifts, neatly tied up in boxes, that portion of the dinner we had not eaten. There is something delightfully original in that idea. The smiles and bows of our host were succeeded by those of his friend, whom he had sent to escort us safely home. His courtesies did not stop here, for he called on us the next morning to thank us for the honour we had done him in accepting his invitation to dine, — a notable expression of the refinement of Japanese politeness.

The night had grown still more beautiful during the four hours we had spent within, and we caught many interesting glimpses of local colour on our way to the hotel. The air was warm, the sky clear, and the brilliantly-lighted parks were filled by proud Japanese fathers and mothers with their prattling children. Men and women were stopping under the cherry-trees that were in full bloom, gazing upon the sacred blossoms that have been dear to Japanese hearts for so many centuries. We went by one of the temples, standing on a hill, the approach marked by a succession of bright red gateways. Under the light of the moon, this ancient structure, which for ages has been the heaven of aspiration and love for so many hopeful spirits of this land, had an air of the utmost impressiveness. The whole scene made us forget that we had been sitting for four hours on our heels, and called to our minds the fact that we had had one of the most enjoyable experiences of our lives.

MIYAKO ODORI.

MIYAKO ODORI.

WE suddenly found ourselves before the entrance to an unfamiliar by-street, and turned to our guide to inquire the meaning of what we saw. The huge red lanterns hanging in a perpendicular row from two high poles, evidently had a significance about which we were in the dark, and the exhibition of haste, which we observed on the part of these leisurely Orientals, surely was inspired by no everyday event. The girls were looking their prettiest with their hair filled with flowers and their pale grey *kimonos* tied with that magical sash-knot, which is the despair of their Western sisters. Along with them trotted their smaller brothers in bright-coloured flowing robes, their little heads cropped close with the exception of a solitary tuft. Fathers and mothers of sedater age and deportment displayed an eagerness that was equally strong, if more quietly marked.

Our attending coolie informed us that we had hit upon a festival that has particular attractions to the foreign eye. You have probably heard of those sacred cherry-blossoms that are so dear to the hearts of the Japanese, and which, with the chrysanthemum, are their chief floral pride. It is true that meddling foreigners have said that they are not cherry-blossoms at all; but that does not seem to prevent the delicate mingling of pink and white from being a very beautiful flower. It is in the month of April that they are to be seen at their best, and it is then that this æsthetic people assemble in different ways, and touchingly illustrate the part that these flowers play in their lives, — for the Japanese without their cherry-blossoms would not be the Japanese at all. When, therefore, the coolie informed us that all these people were on their way to see the famous cherry-blossom dance, we lost no time in mingling with the throng and following it down the lane-like street.

Everything here was a maze of Japanese forms clad in their daintiest robes, and Japanese faces flushed with eagerness and anticipation. Though æsthetic before everything else, the people have a keen eye for business, and the street was lined with booths full of knicknacks and toys of every kind. And here also were whole families picturesquely seated on their heels, sipping the everlasting tea. Pushing our way through the crowd, we drew up before a platform-like entrance, and were immediately met by one of the attendants, who presented us each with a pair of enormous white duck shoes. If you travel long in Japan, you will become accustomed to this sort of thing, and cease from experiencing any embarrassment or indignation at being requested to remove your foot-gear before stepping on a Japanese floor. The irreverent foreigner, however, unaccustomed to walking around in stocking feet, does not always see things from the Japanese point of view, and it has therefore been necessary at the temples and places of public amusement to have

112

Japanese Forms clad in their Daintiest Robes.

a stock of these ungainly foot-coverings for his benefit. The measure, of course, is a conciliatory one, and is intended to smooth the ruffled feelings of the Westerner without at the same time scandalising the sensibilities of the Japanese. We had had many similar experiences, and so lost no time in incasing our feet in a manner that would insure us entrance into the theatre, even though it might detract a little from our dignity.

In the small lobby in which we found ourselves were a number of Japanese enjoying the national attitude of repose, and quietly waiting for something to turn up. The other end of the room was occupied by a counter on which was displayed a large collection of fans made of artificial cherry-blossoms, similar to those that were afterwards used in the dance. These are exhibited in a large measure for the benefit of the foreigner, who is expected to make generous purchases. All the while we could hear notes of that unmistakable Japanese music coming from beyond a small wooden door, mingled with weird voices and unclassifiable sounds. We began to fear that the dance had begun before our arrival, and that we might miss the best part of the show. We signified our wish to enter by pounding on the small door; but it was securely locked, and those on the other side treated our emphatic demands with oriental disdain. As we had paid our admission fee, we began to get indignant at this kind of treatment; but it is better not to get indignant at such things in Japan. Besides, the explanation was quite satisfactory, as one of the attendants told us that it was a fixed rule never to interrupt the performance by the entrance of new spectators, and, therefore, any one who came late must wait until all was finished. We were pacified when we learned that the dance was now nearly over and would shortly be repeated, and that we would lose nothing by waiting. But we were not the only ones who were impatient. There was one little Jap accompanied by his mother, who, after a careful search finally succeeded in discovering a small crack near the floor, to which he applied his eye in much the same fashion that his penniless occidental cousin watches the progress of a game of baseball; and evidently with the same emotions, if the glances of delight which he occasionally threw towards his mother might serve as indications.

Suddenly the music ceased, and the crowd began to push in. Japanese crowds are particularly noted for their good nature, and our progress into the theatre was the occasion of many sprightly jokes from the local wits, which were evidently very good, for they were received with bursts of laughter. We soon found ourselves in a front seat of a small gallery, with a three-sided stage before us. This gallery was reserved for those from over the seas and for those of the higher classes of Japan. Below in the pit sat those of humbler station, making themselves as comfortable as possible with their cushions spread out on the floor. Spectators who had already seen the performance were leaving the theatre from the two entrances under either end of the gallery, but the eager crowd from without was rapidly filling their places. The faces seemed the same that we had parted with a few minutes before, and they had the same appear-

ance of expectant happiness. Here
and there was a father and mother,
followed by five or six wee ones,
hurriedly rushing around to find the
most convenient place. Apparently
satisfied, they would finally sit down,
begin to chatter and laugh, until suddenly one would notice what he
thought a more advantageous place,
when up they would all scramble
again and hurry on in fear that some
one might forestall them. It sometimes took more than two trials
before they were satisfied, and so,
while we were waiting for the curtain to rise, the gay mass below us
was constantly changing about in the
eagerness of the spectators to gain as
comprehensive a view of the stage as
possible. Each little group was provided with that indispensable adjunct
to happiness, — the tobacco-box. The
occasion meant far more to them than

what took place on the stage; it was a general holiday, and they were there to get as much out of it as possible. There was a continual buzz as the conversation went on, and occasionally from some animated group there would rise a loud shout of laughter, whence we could infer that an oriental funny man had made another appreciated hit. Indeed, the sight below us was so interesting and brought us so in touch with the people themselves, that we almost forgot that there was a more pretentious display to follow, and gazed at the curtain before us in total disregard of the glories that lay beyond.

Suddenly our attention was aroused by the loud clapping together of two pieces of wood; and as suddenly every chattering tongue quietly ceased, and every laughing face assumed an expression of the utmost interest. It was the Japanese substitute for the prompter's bell. The curtain obediently rose, and we settled ourselves for the enjoyment of an oriental performance. Even at the beginning we could see that the Japanese prefer to manage these things in a way of their own, for the orchestra with them is not a mere incident of the performance with which to appease the impatience of the audience between the acts or to drown the weak portions of a faltering tenor's solo. In Japan the orchestra is kept behind the curtain as the chief performer, and comes in as generously for its share of applause. The first thing that caught our gaze, therefore, were two rows of *geishas*, picturesquely ranged on either side of the stage, with *koto* and drums ready for the opening overture. They were all painted and plastered after the usual *geisha* style, their little red and white faces surmounted by towering head-dresses of the ever-present cherry-blossom and wistaria. Dainty is a word that one constantly finds one's self using while speaking of the *geisha*, and none other seems to serve the purpose so well. Those on the left, in their bright *kimonos*, with their little drums shaped like hour-glasses, were in the full daintiness of *geisha* life, while those picking the *koto* opposite, though still very young, could not but bring the pathetic thought that that strange life is a brief one. The whole audience observed the strictest silence all through the opening selection, which was not without its charms, even to unaccustomed ears. Occasionally a small shrill voice would be heard above the steady thrumming of the instruments, and though this could not perhaps be called singing, it had charms for those receptive souls in the pit.

But in the mean while
our attention had been
attracted to the stage. It
had been prettily arranged as
a garden scene, in a way far more re-
alistic and beautiful than the painted
trees and urns which pass for such in
our own theatres. Here we had a
profusion of cherry-blossoms to serve
as a background to the equally pretty
and delicate girls, who now began to
enter from the two doors that had been
previously used by the spectators.
They were in two files, one in which
pale blue and pink predominated,
while the *kimonos* of the others were
of bright red. The faces and head-

gear had been arranged in the same way as those of the musicians, and each held in her hand a cherry-blossom fan. Their entering motion was very slow, consisting of a step forward and a step backward, the time of the music being scrupulously observed. In this way they proceeded up the middle of the stage, where they parted and formed in line on the sides, meeting again in the centre. They were now ready for the dance to begin.

The word " dancing," in its western interpretation, can hardly be applied to the graceful body-motions which satisfy the more subdued taste of the Japanese. The nearest thing that our stage can offer for comparison is the march, more spectacular than artistic, in which glistening helmets and emblazoned shields and swords play so large a part. In place of the knightly helmet these Japanese use their cherry-blossom head-dresses to good effect, while their less aspiring minds are satisfied with a fan instead of a sword. They have large flowing sleeves which they are constantly waving with a motion not too slow to be picturesque, and they can bend their little bodies in a way that their Western rivals have yet to learn. They toss their heads backwards and forwards in a very graceful and captivating way, and make any number of gesticulations with their sleeves, holding them in all conceivable positions in front of the face, back of the head, or stretching them out at arm's length as a bat does its wings. At times the march-ing and counter-marching becomes delightfully confusing, the stage being a mass of slowly-waving colour, from the midst of which a large number of cherry-blossomed crests can be seen and an occasional smiling white-plastered face. The dancers do not show the slightest traces of fatigue, and when the curtain is rung, or to be more precise, clapped down at the conclusion of this first act, they seem as fresh as when it began, and a little disappointed that they are obliged to pause for a short time.

Another clap, and up went the curtain again. The scene-shifters had been working hard during the interval, and produced a charming change for the second act. We thought at first that we were to have an oriental version of a well-known scene of Italian love-making, for here was a Japanese house with bow-windows and balconies that would have delighted the eye of the most fastidious Romeo. But there were only Juliets in this play, and they made, after all, a satisfactory use of the windows and piazza, though they relied simply upon their own charms for their success. Now one tiny form would appear in a window, now one would step upon a balcony, and another somewhere amid the trees would smilingly gaze upon her sister above. There were no carefully memorised speeches of blank verse, but the scene was full of that clever *geisha* sentiment that can be so charming. Each little actor became her own poet, yet there was no need of words to make us feel the happy spirit of romance inspiring her unrestrained heart. The atmosphere of gayety was not confined to the stage but found its way into the delighted souls in the pit, and scarcely had the curtain descended when they seemed to feel it their duty to give a performance of their own. The children began to run about, pull each other by the sleeves, roll around on the floor, — all to the accompaniment of ceaseless tittering and all with the utmost good nature. A wrestling match formed the diversion of one group gathered around two diminutive athletes of local reputation, who were tugging savagely at each other with the utmost disregard of usual athletic rules. The pit was not without gymnasts of its own, who turned somersaults and handsprings in a way that must have shocked the more refined taste of the gliding *geishas*. While all this was going on, the more dignified members of the family were sitting on their heels, smoking their pipes in a stately manner, and occasionally bringing forth materials for a light lunch. This would have a greater attraction than the trials of athletic skill, and even one or two of the most successful turners of the somersault made a pause in their gyrations to watch the progress of the meal.

My attention was so occupied by
the busy throng below, that it was
not until I felt a gentle tug at my
elbow that I was aware that I had a
visitor at hand. I turned and saw a
smiling white-plastered face, surmounted by tall sprays of cherry-
blossoms, gazing up into mine. It
was one of the *geishas*, who had left
the stage and who had quickly selected a foreigner on whom to bestow
her favours. And yet, I like to think
her attentions were not merely of a
perfunctory kind, and that she was
drawn towards me for other reasons
than because it was the way in which
she had been trained. Her actions
surely had not an artificial air, and the
continued smiles which she showered
upon me seemed to be sincere. She
did not feel the least embarrassment,
and kept talking on in her sweet
little voice as though I understood

everything that she said. And a great deal of it was perfectly plain. When, for example, she glanced up into my eyes in such a meaning way and let drop a few dulcet words, could my woman's nature refuse to understand the little flatterer? She was amused

by the ornaments on my hat, and smoothed my hair in a most caressing manner. When she tired of this, she called my attention to a small tray at my side, which I had not noticed before. From this she took a cup of tea in her delicate little hands and offered it to me. I drank it with the utmost readiness, and did not stop to think that it was the bitterest thing that had ever passed my lips. This was the real object of her visit, and with another smile she gathered up her tray and passed on. I gave a sigh as I saw her go through the same thing with another lady not far away, and apparently with the same sincerity and feeling. With an equal tenderness would she clasp her hands, and — crushing stroke to feminine vanity — gaze into her eyes with the same admiration as she had into mine.

And now, for the first time, I noticed that there were several *geishas* in the back part of the gallery engaged in making the bitter potion I had tasted under such romantic circumstances. This is no every-day occurrence, and it has a long history that gives it a far from vulgar interest. Perhaps you think that our "teas" are of native origin, and that they are an invention of modern times ; but you are mistaken. In the sixteenth century there lived a mighty man in Japan, named Hideyoshi, and he it is who must bear the burden of those social functions about which the men say so many unkind things. For in his effort to lighten the cares of state and lessen the tedium of his life, Hideyoshi, after much careful thought, decided on the following plan. He gathered to himself several of the choicest spirits of the realm, to whom conversation was a developed art and wit a perennially flowing spring, and said : " I hereby establish an entirely new form of social diversion to be known as ' tea.' In so doing, I have a careful eye on those who shall follow, and particularly those of other lands, who shall shower their blessings upon me to the end of time. So come, my friends, gather around, and in the words of an unborn poet: giggle, gobble, gabble, and git." Probably this last allusion was a mere pleasantry on his part, and had reference to the degenerate forms in which we should receive the ceremony. Hideyoshi had no feminine hands to assist him, — Japan at that period of its history not kindly favouring budding *débutantes*. He went about it himself in this way. He took a piece of purple silk and carefully cleaned each article to be used, folding and refolding the fabric in a most deliberate manner. He then heated a bowl with hot water and placed in it a spoonful of the green powder that the Japanese call tea. Nothing remained but to put in the boiling water and to serve the bitter result. With a most profound bow he passed this around to his guests, giving each at the same time a small cake with a taste rather suggestive of dry ginger.

The affair was a great success, and was taken up with readily by the most exclusive sets of Japan, and passed into modern times. It is called the " *cha-no-yu*," and the Japanese

regard it with a reverence that makes it almost sacred.

The day was now drawing to a close, and the theatre was gradually becoming dark. The informality of the performance was continued at the next rise of the curtain, when the scene-shifters came out and prepared to arrange things for the last act. They were not visible to the specta-tor, however, because they had on black gowns and black masks, — and because the Japanese have a very lively imagination. But to us, not so happily endowed, these men's sombre costumes did not prevent them from being seen, and we watched them with considerable amusement and in-terest as they solemnly went around, preparing the stage for the finale. Everything was darkened, and when the *geishas* again appeared, they each held a candle in one hand and a spray of cherry-blossoms in the other. Enormous clusters of this flower seemed to fall from the wings in one mass, barely leaving room beneath for the little girls to go through the concluding steps. The dance that followed was even slower than the former, and was accompanied by a still weirder music, the finest we had yet heard in Japan. Everything had an air of strangeness and unreality, and we felt indeed that we were in a different atmosphere than that in which we had spent our lives. Slowly the brightly-clad *geishas* moved around the stage, the white blossoms gracefully waving in the air, and still more weirdly rose the threatening tones of the *koto*.

We were aroused from our enchantment by the gradual descent of the curtain. The spectators for the next performance were already entering, the conversational jabber once more began, and to the accompaniment of the same laughing voices and probably the same jokes, we made our way to the street.

THE RISE AND FALL OF THE
KAKEMONO.

THE RISE AND FALL OF THE
KAKEMONO.

IT was our last night in Kioto. We
had spent the day in the temples,
and though we were somewhat tired,
we still managed to keep up a desul-
tory conversation upon the interesting
things we had seen. Suddenly we
were interrupted by a shy knock.
Before any one had time to prevent it,
a handsome Japanese face thrust itself
through the gradually opening door;

it was immediately followed by the handsome figure of a young man. Perhaps it was because of the good looks that the intrusion was not resented. The new-comer possessed large brown eyes, bushy black hair, and beautiful white teeth, and in addition to this spoke English.

"Can look see some of goods. Have very beautiful things."

This is the way they teach it — or, at least, learn it — at the mission schools.

The speaker continued : Would Madame be so kind as to glance at the charming wares at present gracefully reposing in a pack on his shoulders? They were something out of the usual run, and he had brought them especially for her inspection. To tell the truth, Madame was very tired, and murmured an objection ; but a beautiful face has always touched her artistic sensibilities, and here was one of the finest she had yet seen in Japan. The new-comer seemed to notice this, for he entered without more ado. He immediately dropped to the floor and began to unpack his bundles. We were all soon interested in other things than our visitor's face, for he had hardly begun to display his wares, before we saw something novel ahead. Japanese peddlers usually have an innumerable collection of small boxes, but our friend's were larger and heavier and of a much richer kind. With the usual number of bows and smiles he began to reveal his treasures to our gaze, when we were honoured by the entrance of a small counterpart of himself, who had evidently been waiting outside until the coast was clear. Apparently they were brothers, and together they began to arrange their merchandise in a way to catch the American eye most temptingly.

We had already seen many of those hanging pictures which figure so prominently in Japanese art, but nothing of so delicate a texture as those our visitor now laid before us. They were for the most part representations of religious emblems, but there was one of a more secular kind of which the young man was particularly proud. It was rather large, with a dark background on which was exquisitely embroidered a tall, white cock with head erect, crowing to his heart's content, and strutting about in all the majesty of a flaming red comb.

But this was only a beginning. Evidently our friend had brought these merely to see whether we were people of taste and could properly appreciate the untold treasures he had at his command. In his Mikado's English he informed us that our artistic eye had touched him profoundly and had caused him to call to mind a *kakemono* of unparalleled beauty, that would delight us still more. Whereupon, he ruthlessly folded up the cock with the flaming comb, placed it with the rest on the floor, and set the boy down upon the pile to guard matters until his return. It did not seem to occur to him that this latter act was a slur at our honesty — things are different in Japan, you know.

"Have got house very beautiful *kakemono*. Priest won't sell." So he said, and so we understood him; giving him credit for grammatical correctness, when really he meant "want to sell." Here, we thought, is a touching example of Japanese politeness! Our visitor is so impressed by our appreciation of his embroideries that he is about to show us one of the treasures of the temple, for the sole purpose of gratifying our taste for art. Soon this obliging Oriental returned, bearing a large bundle over his shoulder, which he immediately spread before our astonished gaze, all the while murmuring, as we thought, a repetition of the fact that the priest would not sell. We were further mystified by an occasional reference to a tea-house that seemed to disturb the young man's peace of mind.

However much we may have been puzzled by this, there was no doubt that we had before us one of the most delicate creations of art. Could it be possible that all this was the result of man's labour, using what many of us find so clumsy an instrument as a needle? I have thought long how to give an idea of the skill, the patience, the taste displayed in this piece of tapestry; but who can tell

a blind man
what a rain-
bow is like?
Besides, I do not
yet myself thoroughly
appreciate what it all means, for,
though I have owned the tapestry
for some time, I never look at it
without finding something I have not
seen before. It seems such an inade-
quate thing to say, that it was about
eight feet long and three wide, and
that the figures were worked upon
a grey background surrounded by a
border of black. If you could only
have seen it as it first flashed upon
me that evening, a glorious mingling

147

of the bright Japanese colours of red, black, and white, as yet totally un-dimmed by the nearly two centuries that it had lain, a holy thing, in the Daitokuji Temple at Kioto! There seemed to be some historical scene portrayed, evidently a naval battle, for there were castles and boats and water, and in the distance the sacred mountain of Fujiyama, worked in a rich gold. Over all, with outspread wings, were flying storks, and in the sea were strange fish and monsters. And there were royal crests, sailors, warriors, birds of many kinds, the colours as finely blended in this piece of needlework as in an artist's paint-ing. Later I have had the opportunity to examine it more in detail, and to discover that the castles on the shore are undergoing a siege, the date of the events being that of the ascendency of Hideyoshi. We are sure of this because Hideyoshi himself is there in red armour, and though his face is not more than a quarter of an inch in diameter, the features are easily distinguishable. I have the names of the other officers and castles, with a full description of the event written in choice Japanese by the priest of whom the purchase was made.

For he would sell, after all. As we stood admiring this monument of skill and patience, little thinking that it might be ours, the young man kept up his story about the refusal of the priest to sell, and also his pathetic allusions to the mysterious tea-house. Suddenly, however, he cleared up everything by turning to us despairingly with the words, —

"Please buy!"

Then we at last learned that the priest "wanted" to sell, and that he was driven to this strait by the necessity of raising money for a tea-house adjoining the temple. And we gladly bought. It was with reluctance that the priest gave us this Japanese treasure in return for our

American dollars, for behind the act there is a pathetic story that touches the very heartstrings of the faithful followers of Buddha. It might not be inaptly styled " The rise and fall of the *Kakemono*."

In those good old times when the Mikado was only a picturesque ornament of the community, subject himself to the dictates of some powerful *shogun* or warrior like our friend Hideyoshi ; before the barbarous West with its parliaments and trousers and sense of art-perspective had begun to intrude, a great being ruled in the hearts of the Japanese and filled them with longing and hope and love. He was not a native, it is true ; but the fact that he came from India did not seem to make him any less national, and he was as much at home in this sunny island as in his own snowy Himalayas. To tell the truth, the poor Japanese peasant was not the happiest of mortals in those days ; for we have many stories of the little regard in which he was held by those above him, and the insignificant part he played in the social system. It is not altogether strange, therefore, that this wanderer from the south should have met with a hearty welcome; for his lessons were those of kindness and hope. More than this, he taught the down-trodden serf that life was not a mere matter of unrewarded toil and undeserved suffering, but that it had a gleam of greatness even for him, and that besides there was something beyond. This bearer of glad tidings dwelt in the temples on the hills, and his name was Buddha. It is true that the ungodly Japanese had little stone images of him of which they thought a great deal, and so his religion was an idolatrous one; but for all that they might have done a great deal worse.

For many centuries, therefore, they loved great Buddha, and loved him with all their souls. Every one, from the haughty *shogun* to the little white-

faced *geisha*, found in his spirit a
something which he could find no-
where else, and which resulted in a
stronger and purer life. There was
one, however, who remained proudly
aloof from all this, and regarded
Buddha with a somewhat doubting
eye. This was no less a personage
than the Mikado himself, who, after
all, could not be greatly blamed for
the way he looked upon the new-
comer. For Buddha was not only a
foreigner but a revolutionary character, and expelled a former visionary
something very dear to the Mikado's
vanity. This was the creed of Shin-
toism. Now I hope you will not
embarrass me by asking what Shin-
toism is, for I assure you, that though
I have given the matter some attention I have not yet a clearly de-
fined idea as to what it all means. It
does, however, teach us something

indefinite about listening to the dictates of our hearts, and something definite about following the decrees of the Mikado. It treats this dignitary even more kindly than this, for it goes on to say that he is not a man at all, but a great god moving here among us, — a sacred thing to be worshipped. It supports this claim by a very long and highly respectable pedigree, proving him to be descended in the direct line, without twist or turn, from one Amaterasu, who was a sun-goddess before Buddha came. For Buddha did not trouble himself about the Mikado's genealogical tree, and so the good man had little use for him. During many centuries he treasured up his ill-feeling; but things worked slowly in Japan in those days, and it was a long time before disobliging history gave the Mikado a chance to get even with this iconoclast of the south.

To tell the truth, through all these years the Mikado was not the important personage his ancestry would lead you to suppose. His main occupation was posing gracefully as the head of the state, and for ages this descendant of the sun-goddess was kept in golden chains, a practical prisoner in his own castle. But he still kept his hold on the people, who, by some peculiar inconsistency very noticeable in their religious faiths, firmly believed that story about Amaterasu. This, however, did not in the least affect their warm love for Buddha, of which they gave evidence in many ways. They built many temples, which were approached by a series of handsome *torii*, or stone gateways, and which were regularly attended by priests. But by far the best thing they did was to make these embroidered pictures, one of which I have

155

described at length. Those were emphatically the days of the *kakemonos*, and they are the most telling expressions of the deep-rooted affection with which the Japanese regarded their divine teacher. The works are deeply religious in the most profound sense of the word, and fill the same place in Japanese art that the works of Raphael and Michael Angelo do in Christian painting.

And these old masters had their counterparts in Japan, though but few are known to fame. I fancy, for example, that not many have heard of a certain genius named Tosa Mytzeoki; but he it was who flourished at the middle of the last century and spent three years of his life in making the beautiful tapestry that I now possess. The makers of these *kakemonos* formed a separate class of society, and spent their whole lives in the practice

Handsome *torii*, or Stone Gateways.

of the delicate art. They had no instrument but the needle, and no material but Japanese silk with which to produce these wonderful results. They worked year after year at the beck of grosser spirits than themselves, and of course were poor and unhappy. They did not have the hope of fame that inspires so many artistic souls ; for when a *kakemono* was completed it was immediately laid away in the temple, far from vulgar eyes. Poor Tosa Mytzeoki never dreamed that the result of his delicate toil would some day grace an American drawing-room! It is true that on days of religious festivals the *kakemonos* would sometimes be brought out and used in decorations for the walls, but these occasional exhibitions were a sorry foundation for future fame.

When some nobleman — for the

higher classes alone could afford such a sacrifice — wished to gain the favour of Buddha, he would go to one of these humble artists and give him an order for a *kakemono*. There were two kinds from which he might select, those that were embroidered and those made of paper. The latter were especially abundant, and of all kinds and sizes. Many of them contained merely an autograph done with the brush, — the national pen; for the Japanese have always had a liking for fine handwriting, esteeming excellence in that line a separate art. The figures with which a large number of these paper *kakemonos* are covered are splendid examples of Japanese painting, the scenes being mostly of a historical and religious kind. Buddha and Confucius are the special favourites. The backgrounds are often filled with a host of figures;

I remember one at Kioto, that contains nearly as many faces as Tintoretto's painting in the Doge's Palace at Venice. This *kakemono* is remarkable for other reasons than this, for the work is lifelike and vigorous, and though five hundred years old is well preserved. It is called the "Death of Buddha," and represents the expiring prophet surrounded by worshippers with grief-stricken faces, so vividly depicted that the very air seems filled with lamentation.

For many centuries these *kakemonos* were being collected in the Buddhist temples all over Japan. Then came the memorable year 1868, — a year that marked the close of the Japanese middle ages. The feudal system was abolished, and the whole scheme of government renovated. Now the Mikado emerged from his obscure position as a public official, and began to play more than a sentimental part in Japanese life. The days of the *shoguns* were over, and the Mikado was the Mikado indeed. From this time the misfortunes of the *kakemonos* began. The long-awaited opportunity of the Mikado had arrived. He solemnly sent forth an edict that Buddha had outlived his usefulness, and that the day of his great-great-grandmother, the sun-goddess, had come; the sole religion of the Japanese henceforth was to follow the teachings of his heart, but above all those of the Mikado. So Buddha's occupation was gone. The Japanese were already on that downward path, which was to end in their wearing European trousers under Japanese *kimonos*, and they began to find the Indian prophet a little out of date. And besides, the missionaries had impressed upon their minds that those little stone images were things no self-respecting man would have about him. Many, therefore, decided to do away with these abominations, and follow the teachings of their hearts.

But, though the government was persistent, Buddha was even more so, and was very loath to give up the sway he had secured over the affections of the Japanese. The humbler classes were also blind to the superior virtues of the Shinto Temple, and therefore an interesting struggle began, to see which was the fitter to survive. The struggle is not ended yet, nor is there any great indication that it soon will be. The Mikado himself has confessed the weakness of his own cause, for he has found that the mere listening to the teachings of one's heart and obeying the decrees of the sovereign does not constitute a religion.

He has therefore been obliged to borrow a great deal from his antagonist, and it so happens that the state religion of Japan is a tangled problem. But the masses of the people are still faithful to Buddha, whose temples are increasing every day.

In the midst of all these reforms there was one class on whom the burden rested with a peculiar weight. What was to become of the priests? The Mikado cared no more for these than he did for Buddha himself, and so, while a large part of Japan was listening to the teachings of its heart, these priests wandered in a melancholy way about the temples, at a loss as to what it all meant. Not only this, but they were hungry men, as the governmental supplies had suddenly ceased. The temples were beginning to show the evils of the sentimental tendency of the people,

The Mendicant Priests.

and it was evident that something must be done, or Buddha would have to limp back to India with a lessened appreciation of Japanese hospitality. Thus it was that some one more daring than the rest bethought him of the *kakemonos*. Here were treasures indeed, and moreover here were wealthy foreigners beginning to swarm anxiously to lay sacrilegious hands on everything. You see it was a simple case of sentiment *versus* necessity, and as usual necessity came out on top. The priests must be fed, tea-houses must be built, the temples preserved; the government frowned upon them all. Every time, therefore, that the needs became too pressing to be resisted, a *kakemono* was aroused from its rest of ages, and converted into cash. Buddha was thus given a lease of life once more, while his sacred *kakemonos* were transported to do service in the drawing-rooms of Europe and America.

Many of them were bought up by the Japanese themselves. They are a source of entertainment at dinner parties, where they are brought out for the inspection of the guests in much the same fashion that we display our bric-a-brac or collection of paintings. A careful history of each is kept, which always accompanies it. The more *kakemonos* the Japanese has, and the greater the antiquity of them, the prouder man he is. But the demand for them has occasioned many imitations which are reserved for the benefit of the unsuspecting foreigner. The connoisseur, however, can detect the difference as easily as he can distinguish between a copy and an original.

But the problem is not solved yet. The government has issued another decree, obliging the priests to make an inventory of the treasures of the temple, and to see that no more *kakemonos* are sold. He that has secured one of these works of art, therefore, has great cause for congratulation. But one still wonders what is to become of the hungry priests, and the shamefully-treated prophet of India. The question is made more interesting because Buddha shows about as much indication of returning to his native land as the priests do to begin listening to the teachings of their hearts.

A GLIMPSE OF ROYALTY.

A GLIMPSE OF ROYALTY.

" YOU must go to Nara," they told
us, as soon as we had landed
in Japan. "It is one of the oldest
and most sacred cities of the Empire.
Though now politically of little importance, there are many interesting
things to be seen. There are beautiful groves of cryptomerias, shadowy
roads, crumbling stone lanterns, tame
deer, and many an ancient Shinto

temple. If you do not see Nara, you do not see Japan."

And so on a certain April morning we found ourselves on our way to the southern part of the island.

You have heard much of the sunshine and the flowers, the tea-drinking, and the various æsthetic touches of Japanese life, so it may be somewhat disillusioning to learn that there are other points of view. This thought forces itself upon my mind whenever I think of our watery journey to Nara, —for it rains in Japan. The days can be cold and dark, hotel accommodations can be scanty, and foreigners can take a long and hungry railroad ride, and have impressions that they do not care to put down in a book of travels. We had heard the praises of the journey so rapturously sung, that the rainy mountains, the swollen streams, the dripping trees, the cold, wet, and uncomfortable passengers, struck us with a painful sense of the reality of things. As yet I had experienced only the warm and sunshiny side of the climate, and so, as I stepped from the train that afternoon, and gazed about on the various signs of general discomfort, I could but ask myself, " Is this Japan? "

Yes, it was Japan, and more than that, it was Nara. If I had any reasonable doubt, before me stood the everlasting symbol of things Japanese,— the *jinrikisha* man. He had a melancholy and rainy-weather look, which was increased by the freedom with which he had discarded his usual costume and appeared wrapped in a covering of straw. Such a picturesque equipage and ingenuous attendant look well in a photograph, and can even afford a certain amount of pleasure in a busy city with plenty of daylight and interesting objects as a background; but as I stood there, facing the downpour and a two-mile ride, I began to wonder whether the ancient capital of Japan was such a fascinating study as my friends had promised.

For all that, I crawled in, and my stoical friend began to arrange me with a tenderness of which his face betrayed no sign. He drew a leather robe over my lap, tucked it in to keep out the least intruding drop of rain, drew the top of the carriage completely over and shut me in, much after the way in which my grandmother used to draw her sunbonnet over her face. Everything was dark and mysterious, and had I been of a nervous temperament there would have been much to terrify. I began to wonder how the rest of the party was getting on; but the blind faith that there was a *jinrik-*

isha somewhere back of me could not be confirmed until I had reached the end.

I could feel small streams of water trickling down my neck, and pools gathered in the bottom of the carriage. It began to splash into my face and hands; the wind came pouring in, and a blast occasionally unloosened my lap robe. I was surrounded by

impenetrable darkness, with the exception of a small aperture below,
where I caught sight of a pair of un-
covered legs automatically moving.
I divined that these were the property
of the gentleman who had arranged
me in my present position with such
extreme solicitude, and whose spirit
would have been keenly pained had
he known that so large a portion of
the storm was finding its way into
the carriage. His utter disregard of
himself had a suggestion of the sub-
lime; for, though the day was cold,
he had on hardly more than a covering of straw, and his bare feet went
through the mud and pools with the
utmost indifference. I learned after-
ward that his limited wardrobe was
not so real as apparent, and that his
appearance that afternoon was caused
not so much by poverty as by pride;
for this *jinrikisha* man occupied an

enviable position among his fellows, and had reason to consider himself a favourite of fortune. This is all explained when I tell you that he was the haughty possessor of a pair of European trousers. It mattered little to him that these might have been thrown aside by some more fastidious American, or that the style might have been a little behind the time. They were the chief glory of his life, — and the chief torment too. No one can say how much his melancholy aspect was caused by the fact that fate had heaped such bountiful favours and grave responsibilities on his head, — for he lived under the constant fear that some day he might wear these trousers out. And so, with the true Japanese spirit of economy, he had hit upon an excellent plan against such a contingency, — he resolved not to wear them at all.

This unconscious humourist furnished the only diversion of the ride. Doubtless I passed through many delightful scenes, and might have caught many charming bits of Japanese rural life. I shall never know how those tea-fields looked in that pouring rain, and the plodding Orientals that must have passed are a sealed picture. I could occasionally hear the tall trees swaying and scraping together in the cold breeze, but they were not for the eye. All that I could see was a small square of  mud and water, and the mournful movement of the untrousered legs below. These were very instructive

as object-lessons in domestic economy, but I would have preferred to
have enough landscape to set them
off to better advantage. Such an interesting thing, however, was enough
in itself to keep my spirit up, and I
thoroughly enjoyed the ride, in spite
of the many things I could not see.
My faithful friend unconsciously kept
up a stock of that good humour
which was soon to be called into
play; for when we had reached the
hotel where we were to spend the
night, the guide came gloomily towards us and made the announcement
that the house was full, and that we
would be obliged to find some other
place. He said that he had succeeded
in finding a small Japanese house near
by, and that this was the best that
could be done.

It was still raining hard, the night
was getting dark, and there was noth-

ing for us to do but to take what we could get; and I do not know that we regretted it after all. The approach to the house was not convenient, but the place itself was of the true Japanese daintiness: a tiny affair, with but one story, the earthquakes having been duly considered in its erection. It contained but two rooms, and resembled more a child's play-house than a dwelling. It was furnished with the ever-present white mats that are so prominent a feature of Japanese domestic life. We decided to conform ourselves to our surroundings, and be distinctively Japanese. So, carefully removing our shoes, we sat down on our heels, while the guide departed to see what could be found to eat. This oriental posture is very interesting as an experiment, but I would not advise you to let your enthusiasm carry you too far.

If you have spent hours on the floor
with a child playing with paper dolls,
you can get a good idea of what it
is like. Our first intention was to
spend the whole evening in this way,
and in other respects to do as the
Japanese did, but we soon found that
the effect was mainly valuable as fur-
nishing a few jokes to enliven the
conversation. And when we thought
of eating our dinner after the fashion
of the best Japanese society, we
again became irresolute, and were
greatly relieved when one of the little
musmees returned with American
dishes and American chairs. There-
after we let our attendants look after
the honour of Japan. They amused
us during the progress of the meal by
tying and untying their sashes, — their
chief feminine vanity, — and by indulging in the endless capers and
familiarities permitted to the *musmee*

183

alone. The evening passed rapidly and gaily, and the wind and rain were forgotten in the Japanese dreams that followed the artless speeches and childish pranks of our little entertainers.

A soft, grey light came streaming through the paper panes, and in my drowsy ears I heard the chatter of the *musmees*, telling us that it was morning, and time to be on our way. The storm was not entirely over, though it was indulging in a momentary pause. The water was dripping from the trees, only waiting for the sunlight to pierce through the heavy clouds to clothe every leaf with sparkling gems. The sky had an air of indefiniteness and unconcern, in doubt whether to repeat its performance of the day before, or to burst forth into that splendour with which we were more familiar. There was nothing

Tying and untying their Sashes.

lacking but this for a perfect day ; the wind had worn itself out during the night, the atmosphere was assuming a more oriental gentleness, the flowers were fresh and bright, and our hearts were full of gay anticipation. We had little time during the day and evening previous to think of one great predominant fact : that we were at the far-famed city of Southern Japan, warm with tradition and beauty, its history alive with the early tales of a struggling people, its temples and shrines aglow with much that is finest in human sentiment.

We were surprised at our break-fast by the hurried entrance of our guide. He was a man of considerable refinement and composure, and we were therefore taken aback at the excitement that he now displayed. With bated breath he explained to us that the unforeseen had happened, though whether this was a matter of congratulation his demeanour did not make clear. If you are familiar enough with the mixture of reverence and love with which the Japanese regard their dowager Empress, you will readily understand the agitation of our guide. She is an exalted being, the wife of one Mikado and the mother of another, and is besides a most estimable woman with lovable qualities of her own. So when the guide learned that she was at the present time at Nara and would be there for the rest of the day, his emotions of loyalty and awe had a sudden inspiration, and there was nothing for him to do but to try to communicate them to us. After we had satisfied him that we were duly impressed by the situation, he consented to descend to particulars. One of the most ancient ceremonies at

188

Nara is the sacred dance which is yearly given in the adjoining grounds of one of the temples, and at which some member of the royal family is expected to be present. That her

Majesty should select the very day that we had appointed to visit the place can only be considered as a happy coincidence of fate. Preparations had been going on for many days, and everything was ready for a most elaborate performance. At this point the guide became somewhat mysterious, and began to hint that possibly after the royal party had finished we might persuade the priests to repeat the dance for our benefit. Of course we were duly shocked that any such thing should be done, but we smothered our reverential emotions, and decided to make the attempt. I all along suspected that our friend had completed arrangements before he had spoken to us, but he betrayed no evidence of this in his anxiety lest his plan should fail. To confess the truth, I did not feel quite at ease over the matter, for the Empress had been painted to me in a rather unpleasant light, and I was very much afraid of offending her royal pride. I had been told that she regarded foreigners with an unfriendly eye, and was jealous of the innovations that were creeping in from the West, and gradually making the real Japan a thing of the past. It was said that she looked upon the European costume as a thing to be abhorred, and the silk hat as a sign of barbarism. Particularly, my friends had been kind enough to inform me that she regarded the American race as a peculiarly unpleasant growth, and one to be tolerated by no respectable Japanese. Though I discovered later that my information was wrong, the thought sufficed to make me uncomfortable, and I felt that to intrude upon a ceremony intended only for the royal eye, was audacious and indelicate. The assurance of the guide that this had been done before did not mend the matter, and I had some twinges of conscience as I stepped into the *jinrikisha* awaiting to conduct me to the temple grounds.

As we rode out of the court-yard, we observed an interested throng gathered around an equipage of a

kind somewhat difficult to classify.
Had we seen it in an American city
we should have taken it for a dilap-
idated victoria; but it was hard to
determine what connection such a
disreputable affair could have with
the mother of the Mikado. The
whole thing, from the ragged uphol-
stering to the rickety wheels, had
a most unroyal appearance. The
small, shaggy horse may have been
having a good time, but he failed to
reveal it by any expression of contentment. The coachman, however,
managed to extract much satisfaction
from the situation. He had the
bristling, black hair so characteristic of
the people, and on the back of this
he wore a small, low-crowned derby
hat, gracefully cocked on one side,
with an air of great self-satisfaction.
His dress was the not uncommon
combination of Japanese *kimono* and

European trousers, the latter being carefully creased, and turned up to display his American shoes. His studied attempt to appear dignified was made the more amusing by the shortness of his stature; but the crowd was not amused. The Japanese take this sort of thing seriously, and the only emotions their faces displayed before this cosmopolitan outburst were those of envy and admiration. When my attendant informed me that this was the equipage provided for the first lady of Japan, I began to suspect that her reported dislike of western civilisation was unreal. I told the *jinrikisha* man to hurry on before she came out, as I was anxious to escape her observation.

We entered the temple-grounds by a long avenue arched over by tall cryptomerias, which extended in a tangled forest on either side. Through the wistaria vines, almost as dense as a jungle, occasional glimpses of the sky could be seen. There was little sunshine, and the morning had the air of twilight. The avenue extended in a long and regular line ahead, and seemed a fitting entrance to the most sacred shrine of Japan. A gentle touch was given the whole scene by a number of tame deer that find safe abode in these forests, where the hunter is unknown. As they came up to us and looked into our faces with their large, confiding eyes, they were followed by a troop of little girls who had cakes to sell, of which the animals were very fond. Little was said, for we all felt that we were in a sacred atmosphere, and the quieting influence of the past was beginning to steal over us. The endless array of those famous stone lanterns, ranged on both sides of the avenue,

was a fitting suggestion of former
glory ; the days of many of these had
long gone by, and they were slowly
crumbling in ruins. We were told
by our guide that oc-
casionally one was
lighted, but most of
them had been ex-
tinct for years. Be-
fore us we could see
the pavilion where the
dance was to take
place. It was a sim-
ple roof supported by
columns, its floor the
mat - covered earth.
The priests were walk-
ing around in their
stately white robes and fly-screen
shaped hats, with little priestesses by
their side. We had abandoned our
jinrikishas on entering the grove, and
now walked slowly along, thinking

of nothing but the trees, the stone lanterns, the deer, and the general beauty of the scene. Even the Empress had been forgotten, until, happening to glance back, I was startled to see the royal carriage with the sedate coachman on the seat, ambling along at a leisurely Japanese gait. A few seconds later it stopped, and the Empress and her retinue alighted, with the apparent intention of doing the rest of the journey on foot. Wishing to avoid observation, we quickly stepped behind one of the stone lanterns at a turn of the road. Unfortunately we were not quick enough, or the glance of her Majesty was too keen, for our presence and hurried movement did not escape her. As she slowly passed we had a good opportunity to observe her closely, and in spite of the disagreeable stories we had heard, the impression was

not an unfavourable one. She was
apparently seventy years of age, with
an intelligent and kindly face, having
by no means the severe demeanour
we had been led to expect. She
was dressed in the old-time Japanese
style, with bright red skirt and white
satin *kimono*. Her hair was arranged
in a kind of a halo, falling down her
shoulders in the back. All the ladies
in her train were dressed in a similar
style, but the men were attired after
the European fashion, — in the prevail-
ing court costume. The chamberlain
of the household department, an
elderly man, was in charge of affairs.
As the procession neared our place
of vantage, it turned to the right in
the direction of the Temple-grounds.
We were about to congratulate ourselves that we were to escape unseen,
when her Majesty turned completely
around and subjected us to a scrutiny

that was embarrassing, however kindly meant. I bowed with a reverence that would have done credit to the most obsequious Oriental, and at the same time the men of the party lifted their hats in approved occidental style. The ladies and gentlemen of the royal retinue returned our greetings with a politeness that rivalled our own, but the Empress did not incline her body in the least. She continued gazing at us with the same puzzled expression, yet with no indication of displeasure. Apparently satisfied with what she had seen, she presently passed on. The few moments had been embarrassing for us, for we did not know of how many breaches of propriety we might have been guilty ; and our salutations had not been without a touch of penitence as well as respect.

The Empress had hardly disappeared when one of the priests, with long robes waving in the wind, came running towards us. We were now confident that he had some message from the Empress, and were fearful that the long-expected dislike of foreigners was to be shown. This idea could hardly have been gained from the priest's face, however, as it betrayed no evidence of offended dignity, though there were signs of anxiety and surprise. He paid no attention to us, but immediately engaged our guide in an earnest conversation, the conclusion of which we waited with some apprehension. Finally our attendant turned and spoke to us in the following surprising terms, —

" Her Majesty has learned with pleasure that you have come so far to see the sacred dance, and is very glad that you have happened here the same day as herself. She is very unwilling, however, that you should be kept standing while she witnesses the performance, but thinks that you should be treated with all the kindness and hospitality of Japan. She has therefore sent one of the priests to bid you greeting, and offers you the seats that have been prepared for herself and party; and she will feel very much offended if you do not accept."

These words affected us with mingled feelings of astonishment, flattery, and embarrassment. We had heard much of the politeness of the Japanese, but here was a unique expression of it; one could hardly receive more. And what had become of the dislike for foreigners which I had been told was so prominent a trait in her character? We were somewhat in doubt as to what was the right thing to do, and stood there gazing at each other for a few moments, waiting for some one to take the initiative.

"I hope you will thank her Majesty for us," I finally answered, "but we could not think of taking her place at the dance. We can just as conveniently wait until she has finished. We all, however, very deeply feel her kindness."

"Oh, but you must come — you must come," hurriedly returned the guide, dropping a little of his formality in his fear that we would not accept. "The Empress would not like it at all if you refused her invitation. She says that she can see it at any time, but you have come from far over the seas, and must see it to-day or never. You cannot decline, — it would never do."

Without considering the possibility

of our refusal any further, he and the priest immediately led the way. There was nothing for us to do but to follow; and the faces of our Japanese friends were wreathed in smiles as they saw that we had overcome our scruples. We were much relieved on our arrival to find that the Empress and her train had gone to the northern part of the temple to perform their devotions. However much we would have liked to thank her in person, our acquaintance with Japanese court etiquette was not such that we could know just how it should be done. With a genuine oriental awe we seated ourselves in the chairs that had been destined for the venerable Empress, and from the cups made for nobler hands drank the tea that was meant for royal lips. We soon found ourselves in a more comfortable frame of mind, and by the time the dance had begun, we were in a condition to enjoy it.

There is not much variety in Japanese dancing, and that which we saw on this occasion differed little from many similar performances we had attended. There were five little girls, ranging from nine to twelve years of age, dressed in the old imperial costume of red silk, with divided skirts, the white *kimono* being covered by another of gauze, painted with purple wistaria. As usual, their faces were covered with white plaster, their lips were of a bright carmine, and their eyebrows shaved. Their hair, tied in gold paper, hung down their backs, and on their foreheads were clusters of wistaria and white camellias. The accompaniment was furnished by two priests, one performing on a kind of fife, the other provided with two small sticks of wood, which he struck together, at the same time that the chief priest delivered, in a high-pitched voice, notes very suggestive of the Midway Plaisance. The dancing consisted of the slow posturing that the Orientals so much prefer to the agile movements of the West, and we had begun to catch the spirit of it, and were able to enjoy it after the true Japanese style.

We saw no more of the Empress who so disliked foreigners, but who could treat them with such delicacy. We had another indication of her kindly disposition, however, after we had left the pavilion at the conclusion of the dance. Outside stood the sacred white horse always to be found near these ancient temples, and one of the little girl attendants stood by, selling the peculiar mixture which forms his only food. After I had done my duty by the divine animal,

I took the hand of the little girl, who looked up into my eyes and said, —

"Her Majesty has just gone by. She was very gentle to me, and gave the sacred horse many measures of grain."

FIN DE SIÈCLE JAPAN.

FIN DE SIÈCLE JAPAN.

YOU must not think that you are a person of no consequence if you do not receive an invitation to the Mikado's garden-party, for there are a great many important people not always on his Majesty's list. I cannot tell you just what are the necessary qualifications to the royal favour, for the presence of the entire diplomatic corps is not always requested, the pride of many a native noble receives a fall, and no one knows what anguish of mind the majority of the democratic Americans in Yokohama experience at not receiving a card. Perhaps the most fortunate thing connected with the party is the delicate flower that is its most prominent feature; everything in Japan connected with the cherry-blossom is sacred, and this probably accounts, to some extent, for the chariness with which the Mikado distributes his favours. In October the advent of the chrysanthemum is similarly observed, but this function is not as important as that held in April. Everything depends on the capriciousness of the cherry-blossom, and the party is given early or late as the pink and white deign to display themselves to the worshipping Japanese. Invitations, therefore, are issued only a few days in advance, and are then subject to recall should circumstances happen to prevent the spring-time flower from looking its daintiest.

The invitation is written in highly-refined Japanese with a sixteen-petaled chrysanthemum crest in gold. The party is held in the royal Asakusa garden, and the Mikado is always present with his slim, pretty little wife at his side. The guests are usually very punctual in assembling; the national anthem is played with a royal sonorousness; the Emperor and Empress, with a dignified suite, pass through the garden with the genuine stolidity of ceremonial Japan. Presentations are seldom made, and when there is a person of sufficient dignity and importance for this honour, the ceremony is more stately than cordial. The larger part of the time is spent in admiring the cherry-blossoms, which are everywhere, and which in their early glow are of singular beauty. All this is very well; yet it is not the Mikado or the flowers

that are likely to attract the greater
part of your attention. There is a
feature of the party of more surpass-
ing interest than these: this is the
high hat. It is this picturesque head-

piece which redeems the sombreness of
the gathering, and makes it an event
unique in social life. You are probably somewhat surprised that our occidental high hat and the delicate white
and pink cherry-blossom of Japan
should have anything in common, but

they do have a great deal. Several years ago the Japanese saw that this article of dress was the very thing needed to crown gracefully their *kimono*-clad forms, and they eagerly took it. They borrowed it of course from western foreigners, for the Japanese imagination is not capable of such wild flights as this. It has so become the fashion that they now regard it with a kind of reverence, and require its appearance on the most sacred occasions. It is therefore specially stipulated in the Mikado's invitations to his parties that the gentlemen shall wear frock coats and high hats. The ladies are left to their own judgment, and generally appear in light calling dresses.

But this stipulation has been the cause of no end of dismay to those foreigners so ambitious of social advancement in Japan. The American is more likely to suffer in this respect than his European cousins. At any rate it not unfrequently happens that when sailing for the land of the *kimono* you leave your high hat on western shores. And so an invitation to the Mikado's party affects you with mingled feelings of apprehension and tickled vanity. It is a case where a beaver hat can be quite a serious affair. At first you give up in despair, and decide that the invitation must be declined, but on second thought you think it might be well to consult your confidential Japanese friend. You are somewhat relieved when this gentleman assures you that everything can be arranged, and that there is nothing to prevent your attending the party, — and in a high hat too. The Japanese friend now murmurs something about "The Beaver Pound," and you immediately recall certain institutions at home where stray animals are gathered from their wanderings, and protectingly held until the require- ments of the law are fulfilled. You are a much puzzled man ; but after you have been conducted to the place mentioned, this state of mind is likely to give place to another. With the utmost gravity your friend discloses

to you the treasures of the place, and politely invites you to help yourself. For here are high hats, both silk and beaver, of all sizes, ages, and countries, and you must be a very fastidious person indeed if you find nothing to your taste. Every time a westerner

215

leaves a high hat behind him it is immediately spirited away by mysterious hands, and it is seen no more until it graces the head of a careless foreigner at some social occasion of more than common import. By this time there is quite a collection, ragged and marred as the coins and stamps that are a frequent hobby with us.

You had better visit the Pound early, as the hats are in great demand, and you may have difficulty in fitting your head. You finally make a choice; the likelihood being at best that you will have a size too large or small, but this is only the simplest of the complications. You are by no means the first man that has worn this hat, and it shows the effects of many cherry-blossom parties. Occasionally a new sleek hat finds its way into the Pound, and there is considerable competition as to who shall secure the prize. You had better in some way exhaust all the humour that the idea gives you before you attend the party, else you will not have sufficient command over yourself to view the occasion with the stoical eye of the Japanese; for the hats show off to a better advantage from a comparative point of view. You must place a neat, decorous, low crown of the latest style beside the parabolic curve of several years ago to see really how funny it all is. There is the white and drab head-piece, suggestive of the gentleman of sporting tastes, and an occasional shaggy something that we now see only in pictorial representations of Uncle Sam. All this is very amusing; but it is a graver matter when a young man of eighteen has to parade around in a widower's weed, or a staid clergyman or pompous Member of Congress is obliged to hide behind the

trees in order to conceal the fact that
his head is adorned by one of the
little peaked affairs in vogue a long
time ago. Nor are these the only
things in the same line. The ladies
of the court have caught that disease
which is spreading so rapidly in Japan,
— Europamania, — and have cast
aside their beautiful native costumes
for a western dress. Their success at
best is doubtful, but there is one who
seems to have managed things with
a greater skill. You will likely wonder how the Mikado's wife can look
so well when you have heard of the
difficulties she has to undergo in her
desire to dress like a European lady.
Her person is too sacred to be touched
by vulgar hands, and this unfortunate fact interfered with her progressive plans for some time, until the
problem was solved by fitting her
dresses upon one of her attendants

of similar height and figure. In spite
of this inconvenience, the Empress
appears very well, and is one of the
few Japanese ladies who wears the
European costume with dignity and
grace.

Yet all this is only a fair example
of what you may see in any part
of Japan. The changes that have
been sweeping over the country have
not been confined to political institutions, but have affected the most
trifling details of Japanese life. It
makes no matter where you go, or
the people you meet, everything bears
the traces of the new lands and peo-
ples that have found such favour in
their eyes. To any one who has a
taste for the picturesque, the attempts
of the Japanese at cosmopolitanism
are an interesting field of study. The
background of their life is, of course,
the Japan of ages gone by, with its

Mikado, its flowers, its sunshine, and its tea; but upon this are sprinkled the innumerable foreign traits that make everything grotesquely amusing. With their Mikado they have parliamentary government, and though they are perhaps as fond of their tea as ever, they can occasionally lay it aside for the champagne of the West, and beer flows almost as freely as in Germany itself.

We Americans may take a pride in all this, and may feel delighted that the Japanese will christen themselves with such names as George Washington and Abraham Lincoln; yet I have my doubts whether it is not a mistaken idea of development that persuades us to dignify it by the name of progress. The Japanese are extremely quick and imitative, but like most imitative people, they are likely to perceive only what is most obvious, and so become grotesque. They can see that there are many attractive things about the feminine attire of the West; they fail to see that it is not suitable to themselves. It is a question, after all, whether it is the preferable qualities of the new things which they meet that leads them to adopt them, or whether it is a mania simply for what is new. At the best they are in a stage of transition. The East is constantly touching the West, and the average Japanese to-day is an interesting combination of the inherited traits and emotions of a remote civilisation, and an environment too powerful to be resisted.

You will understand all this immediately, should you take a short walk in one of the streets of a representative Japanese city. The appearance of the people will strike you as un-Japanese. The women, as a rule, do not now blacken their teeth, or shave their eyebrows, as you have been brought up to suppose. There are still, it is true, many who do not like to see these usages die out; but most of them live in the country districts, which have naturally not been affected by the changes in the same way that the cities have. The old women still go around with blackened teeth, but it is because they were disfigured this way before the innovation was introduced. The Empress adopted the new idea a few years ago, and the people have rapidly followed. Most of the women still wear the dress of their ancestors, yet it is doubtful whether this is by inclination or necessity; anything in a foreign line is a luxury, and only the higher classes can afford to follow the style. They still retain their peculiar ambling walk, which is like a slow run, but there are many little indications that this will be abandoned soon.

It is in the dress of the men, however, that the greatest changes are to be seen. The number of combinations that the average Japanese can ring upon *kimono* and coat and trousers, I have never yet tried to count, but you cannot go into a city street without seeing a new one. It is sometimes the *kimono* and trousers, sometimes the trousers without the *kimono*, or the *kimono* without the trousers. They view the derby hat with great favour, and some wear their hair long, like an American football player. They have caught the infection of creased trousers, and take satisfaction in rolling up the ends of them in the clearest weather. I once saw an enthusiastic and progressive Jap walking stolidly through the streets with a small stiff hat perched on the back of his head, with his *kimono* turned up in the back, disclosing a pair of flannel underdrawers, white stockings, and laced American shoes, the whole gracefully consummated by a cane, which he swung jauntily as he marched along. The conscious pride that he took in this outfit was something delightful to see, and the serious and possibly envious glances showered upon him by his friends showed that he was a centre of admiration.

I was surprised one day by a vehicle that I saw slowly creeping up one of the streets of Tokio. It was a small affair, with a single horse in front, the approach of which was announced by the mournful jingle of a bell. At a distance the equipage looked like a little yellow box, and it was some time before I could convince myself that it was a sorry specimen of that most American of institutions, — a horse-car. I learned later that it was only Tokio that could boast of such an incongruity, and the contented and proud air of the driver was in itself an indication that his position was an unusual one. It was rather the idea of the thing that was so delightful, for so far as convenience was concerned, the slow motion of the car could not be thought much of an improvement over the *jinrikisha*.

I have a Japanese friend who had been educated in America and had adopted our ways, who relates an amusing experience he had in connection with this strange innovation. The cars have bells and conductors after the American plan; but, unlike our custom, they are used for the purpose for which they are designed. My friend did not know this, and so when he wished to alight he walked out to the platform and jumped off while the car was in motion. He had not gone far, however, when he saw the conductor running frantically after him, with an air of the utmost consternation. The car was stopped, and quite a crowd collected to watch the outcome of the dispute. My friend was astonished, and completely in the dark as to what it all meant, when the conductor in angry tones asked him how he dared to disregard the law by alighting from a horse-car while it was going at full speed? The accused man protested his ignorance of such a statute; but the conductor was unpacified, and threatened to call a policeman. It was only when he learned that his unruly passenger had lately returned from America, where they do all kinds of barbarous things, and where he had learned to disregard the conductor, that he consented to let him go. My friend received a solemn warning never to repeat the act, and on so promising was reluctantly released.

Many other things in the streets will remind you of home. It is nothing strange to see a bicycle come leisurely down the street, perched upon by a Jap clad in the combination of trousers and *kimono* that most strikes his fancy. The electric light is rapidly being introduced. The Japanese have their policeman, and they dress him after the European style. He has a blue uniform, a small peaked hat, and a club, — but here the comparison must

227

cease. He does not exactly know what to do with all the power bestowed upon him, and he will never arrest a man except on extreme provocation. When he does decide to enforce the dignity of the law, he calmly goes up to his prisoner, ties his hands together with a hempen rope, and leads him off with the utmost gentleness.

The English language suffers at the hands of our commercial friends, and their attempts to catch the American trade in this way reveal many startling things. One shop informs us that " cakes and infections " are found within ; but the best thing in this line I have seen, is the following business card of a Yokohama firm : " Jewelry maker, a finest in town, Whiskey Boy. Our shop is best and obliging worker that have everybody known, and having articles genuine Japanese crystal and all kinds of Curious Stones, Shells, Ivory Cats-eyes — work own name on mono-grams or any design according to orders. We can works how much difficult Job with lowest price insure, please try, once try. Don't forget name Whisky."

English, however, is spoken fairly well, and with what Japanese he will pick up, the average foreigner gets along without much trouble. There has been lately introduced that ever-present travelling companion, the phrase-book, in which we are told how to ask the time of day, what we want for dinner, and other needful questions; but the language is so strange in its construction, that few have courage to try anything very elaborate, and for more intricate mat-ters must rely upon the guide, who usually speaks our language with

fluency. One of the men of our party tried on a certain occasion to show a little gallantry to his attending *geisha*, and began to tell her, by the aid of a phrase-book, that she had very beautiful eyes. He thought that he had succeeded so well in this that he would go one step further, and presumed to inform her that they shone like the stars. You will see that this latter is not only a more delicate compliment, but that it is a more involved sentence, and requires knowledge of grammatical construction not essential to the more simple statement. The little *geisha* did not understand him at all, but he kept at it persistingly almost the entire evening. Finally the interpreter was called in, and the puzzling speech was rendered into Japanese. The girl glanced coyly up and replied: "Oh, but there are a great many favoured in the same way." After that our friend gave up the phrase-book, and conducted his future gallantries by means of an interpreter.

The Japanese have learned more things from the visits of foreigners than a change of costume and the art of war. Perhaps the spirit of trickery is inborn, but the numerous signs we saw of this were of an order that would do credit to the shrewdest Yankee. One of our party was always

a little sensitive to any reference to
ducks, and I myself had an experience
with certain artistic representations of
dragons of which I was frequently
reminded by my friends. Our companion, while taking an evening walk
in Kioto, had been attracted by a certain individual carrying, by means of
shoulder straps, a miniature pond, in
which there were very dainty images
of ducks swimming around as naturally as you could wish. He paused
to watch the proceeding, and became
deeply interested. His enthusiasm
reached its height when he saw the
fowls occasionally dive under the
water and reappear, apparently greatly
refreshed by the plunge. My friend
excitedly asked the price of these
phenomenal birds, paid down a large
sum with great willingness, received
a paper with instructions as to the
way to produce the desired effect, and

started for the hotel. Arriving there, he began to read the paper in order to prepare for the first exhibition. He was somewhat chagrined by being advised therein to buy a few sprightly gold fish, attach them to the ducks, place both on the water, and await developments.

And now, I suppose, it would be only fair to tell you how I was victimised by a similar piece of roguery. I had not been in Japan long enough to distinguish the good shops from the bad, nor to know the proper methods of collecting curios. I was attracted one morning by a graphic representation of a woman sitting on a dragon, the whole evidently the work of a Japanese sculptor. The colour of the image, a rich dark brown, was what particularly struck my fancy. The keeper of the shop in-formed me that it was a rare piece of art, that it was made of a certain sacred wood, and that the price was thirty dollars. I did not buy that morning. In the evening we took a walk through one of the busy streets, and lo! here was an itinerant merchant with my dragon at his side, anxiously looking for a customer. I quickly stepped up to him, and listened to the same tale I had heard in the morning, with one important exception,— the price was now eighty-five cents. Perhaps because I thought I was getting a bargain, perhaps out of curiosity, I purchased the statue, had it done up in paper, and departed with my treasure. Before I showed it to my friends I thought I would wash it a little, as it had a very dusty look, and would be improved by a bath. I was somewhat startled to see the rich dark brown colour fade away and leave me a pure white dragon of a cheap Japanese material resembling plaster-of-paris. I called in the guide, who gave a broad grin as he surveyed the melancholy object before me. He kindly told me that it had been " dipped in medicine," and I made him a present of the curiosity for his information. He bore it away with a satisfied air, and that was the last I saw of my dark brown dragon, — though by no means the last I heard of it.

These are only a few of the ways in which the influence of the West can be traced in Japan. It will be interesting to watch what the next few years will bring about ; whether the

kimono will triumph over the trousers,
the tea over the beer, or whether there
will be a gradual mingling into a new
type. The whole thing may be but a
temporary mania, a passing aberration
of a quickly assimilative people; and
perhaps in a few years the progressive
Japanese will see the folly of his ways,
and learn that he can best advance
after a manner of his own.

CHO AND EBA.

CHO AND EBA.

THEY were surely not the most dis-
tinguished friends we made while
we were in Japan. As far as worldly
considerations went, they were very
humble indeed ; but they possessed
other qualifications which entitled
them to our favour, and the youthful
Eba particularly has left a lasting impression on our minds. Throughout
our stay they were our companions;
we could never visit a temple without their aid, nor climb a mountain

without their words of advice and encouragement. On many a shopping expedition did they faithfully act as our guides, and many a quiet hint would they give us as to the commercial wiles of their countrymen.

Cho and Eba belonged to the most insignificant class of oriental society. In a land where caste is of such importance, I know that any of our aristocratic Japanese friends would be horrified to learn that we entertain so kindly a remembrance of these paltry creatures, to whom the haughty noblemen of the East would hardly deign to give a passing glance. Perhaps it was because we treated them differently that they repaid us with such tender regard and would apparently sacrifice any happiness of their own to give us a momentary satisfaction. For our humble friends were *jinrikisha* men, and, more than that, they belonged to the despised class of the coolies. Before you have travelled long in Japan you will become very familiar with the two-wheeled conveyance which has become an institution of the country, and will take a patriotic interest in it, for it is reported to be the invention of an American. It is a low carriage with shafts, in which a toiling coolie acceptably fills the place of a horse, and it is preferred by the Japanese to the most elaborate coach-and-four of the West. It was for this position in the world that Cho and Eba were born, and in this capacity they proved indispensable to us.

It was at our landing that we met them for the first time, and had our first *jinrikisha* ride. As you step upon the soil of Japan, you will see a long row of these carriages with shafts resting on the ground, and at the same time a corresponding row of unobtrusive natives who accost you with a most respectful air. They have been sitting between the shafts, with their hands around their knees, patiently awaiting the landing of the boat, when they know their services will be required to conduct the passengers to the Grand Hotel. They have spent the time in laughing at each other and cracking Japanese jokes, for the amount of merriment they can get out of life seems without end. If the air is cold, they will be wrapped up in blankets, and will remind you of our western Indians; but oftener their covering consists of the simple blue tights which will become so familiar to you in the days to come. If you are so unfortunate as to land on a rainy day, they will throw this aside for a covering of straw with bare feet and legs; but the weather will not affect their spirits at all, and they will sit with the water pouring down upon them, and crack the same old jokes, and laugh with an appreciation to which the sunshine can add nothing. They wear the regulation mushroom hat, with their name and number inscribed across the front.

You will, of course, immediately call to mind the hackmen of the West, but more by way of contrast than comparison. The duties of each are in a large measure the same, but here they are exercised in a way that is entirely different. The Japs have none of the disagreeable aggressiveness of their western contemporaries; they are quiet and polite, preferring, indeed, that you should take the initiative in the transaction. It is very interesting to watch the outcome of a rivalry that sometimes occurs when two of the coolies hit upon the same patron. The angry dispute to which

many of us are accustomed never takes place; they treat each other to smiles instead of scowls, and the unsuccessful aspirant leaves with a laugh to find a more appreciative customer. During my stay in Japan I hardly ever saw a discontented or angry *jinrikisha* man, and if a genial smile and gentle manners are an indication of inward happiness, they are the happiest mortals it has been my lot to meet.

All this is very well, and yet it is with some hesitation that you decide to surrender yourself into the care of one of those unpromising equipages, and it was my first impulse to look around and see if something less oriental could not be had ; but I quickly reproved myself, and remembered that I was in Japan. Meanwhile, my companion had arranged the matter, and I saw a little old man smilingly approaching, dragging the dreaded *jinrikisha* behind him. His face was sadly wrinkled, his moustache was small and grizzled, and when he lifted his hat I saw that his hair was white. His spirit, however, seemed very buoyant, and not to have suffered from the many years of toil that would occasionally make his step a little un-steady. I felt a natural hesitation about permitting this little old man to drag me about the city; but the almost pa-ternal air with which he assisted me into the carriage made me feel more at ease. Glancing at his cap, I saw that my new acquaintance bore the name of " Cho."

I had hardly been comfortably seated when I saw my companion ride past, borne by much nimbler and more youthful legs than those of my poor old Cho. Riding in Japan is the most unsocial thing in the world. Each traveller has a *jinrikisha* to himself, and the carriages are compelled by law to move in single file, so that the streets may not be blockaded. It is true that they will sometimes hold more than one person; but these con-veyances are meant for the Japanese alone, who are so light that two can be carried by one man. The constant parade of the *jinrikishas*, therefore, through a large thoroughfare, is very interesting. It makes no difference how many people there may be in your party; one must follow another in regular order, or your offending coolie may find himself in the lock-up before the day is over. You can easily see the disadvantages of this state of affairs; it makes conversation almost impossible, — and who can travel with pleasure if he cannot talk?

Both for this reason and for another, which I afterwards learned, I soon lost sight of my companion, whose more sprightly attendant speedily left my veteran in the background. Cho made little effort to gain a position ahead of his fellows, but leisurely fell into line, and trotted along with the contentment of old age.

247

As I knew that my forerunner was looking for rooms, I was not greatly annoyed.

I arrived at last, bringing up the rear; and as we stood there congratulating ourselves, the younger man slowly approached us. Eba had a face of unusual intelligence, and his eyes sparkled in a way that contrasted forcibly with the dreamy blinking of Cho. His whole appearance was less conservative. Under his *kimono* he wore something that had a resemblance to western trousers, and he had discarded the mushroom-hat for a peaked cap like that of a college student. His every feature bore evidence of a keen though kindly disposition; his hair was thick and wiry, his eyebrows heavy, his mouth large and firm. He had a way of darting sharp glances at you that immediately let you know that here was a man who

was not likely to bring up last in a
'rikisha or any other race.

He bowed profoundly, with a smile,
and said, —

"Please you have me to-morrow."

My companion murmured that he
might if he was a good man.

"Oh, yes; me very good man.
Can run fast."

"What is your name?"

"My name Eba; can run very
fast."

He had already given evidence of
this, and he was told to be on hand
the next morning. He bowed again,
and moved on. But he had an un-
satisfied air, and in a hesitating way
he turned around and approached us
once more.

"Cho, you know," he said, with
an anxious though somewhat down-
cast face, "Cho very good man
too."

And he looked at me appealingly.

"Yes," I returned, "Cho is a very good man."

"Cho not quick like me," he returned, somewhat reassured; "but a very good man. Cho old."

After he had given us this information he waited for a few moments, meditatively digging his bare toes into the sand. Finally he came to the point.

"Me bring Cho to-morrow? Very good man. My friend."

We told him that we would be very glad to see Cho also; and with a face beaming with smiles, and the most exaggerated of bows, Eba took his leave.

This was the beginning of our acquaintance with these two friends, and we grew to be very fond of them during the weeks that followed. They were most assiduous in their atten-

tions, devoting to us all their time.
The first thing we saw every morning
as we glanced out of the window,
were the forms of our coolies gracefully reposing in their shafts, waiting
until it was our pleasure to take a
ride. Eba was of a light-hearted temperament, and was always laughing
and joking with Cho, who received
his advances with a sedate air more
suited to his greater age. We had
already had a touching example of
the filial care with which the younger
looked after the older man, and this
was only one of many. I tried several
times to learn whether there was any
particular relationship which necessi-
tated this attention, but never discovered that there was anything beyond
a congenial sense of comradeship.
We may be sure that Cho was not
the only one who profited by this,
for Eba was of a more impulsive

nature, which might have done many
foolish things had it not been for the
sage advice of his senior. He always
treated him with the utmost respect,
and his attentions were those of an
affectionate son.

I had been frequently told that the
Japanese were a people of little natural emotion, and that their extreme

expression of respect and affection
was merely the national idea of politeness. When I think of this I always
call to mind our two humble friends,
and the genuine attachment I am
confident they still have for us. The

two men's natures were as widely different as their ages ; Cho was the practical man, and thought that the best way he could manifest his affection was by polishing up the *jinrik-isha* wheels to a dazzling brightness, or by running up a difficult hill with unusual rapidity ; but Eba more romantically permitted himself little attentions in the way of Japanese nosegays, and in pointing out unusual and attractive features of the scene. Cho kept a careful eye on our business affairs, would drop many a quiet hint on the practices of the shopmen, and thought that the greatest kindness he could do us was to prevent the impositions of his crafty countrymen. It was evident that he despised the more artistic nature of his companion, and at one time I feared that their friendship might suffer from the little rivalry that was going on.

253

As Eba's nosegays increased in size, our carriage wheels grew brighter and brighter, and when Eba was spending a large part of his time pointing out new and interesting scenes, Cho seemed to be seeking unknown curio shops from which to warn us to keep away.

Eba was more intelligent than Cho, and was always ready to talk. He told me that he could read and write Japanese, having attended school between the ages of eight and twelve. He was twenty-two years old, and had dragged *'rikishas* for about six years. He now worked for a company at three yen a month, but he was working hard, and in time hoped to save up enough money to buy his own carriage and be his own master. In addition to his business capacity, he had a quick eye for what was really fine, and always used the utmost taste in the selection of his bouquets.

On one occasion he was delightfully æsthetic. We had been riding in a suburban district, and the roads were lined with wild-flowers. We paused a moment for a little rest, and lounged around in the grass in various attitudes of ease. I grieve to record that Cho leaned his head against a tree and went to sleep, but I have a better tale to tell of Eba. I could see him wandering around at a short distance, picking now and then a flower, which he arranged with the utmost care. He seemed to bestow a large amount of thought on every fresh addition, rejecting many a posy that he had selected, and starting on a new search for something he had not yet found. Finally satisfied, he returned and presented me with the result. It was a little bouquet not as large as your thumb, but perfect in every detail. It was surrounded by a thin border of green, and the flowers were the tiniest I had yet seen in this land of tiny things. The production was a real work of art, and could never have been accomplished but by a man of inherent delicacy. It seemed almost a sacrilege after this that my tasteful friend should be. subjected to the indignity of lifting the *'rikisha* shafts, and toiling up the steep hills like an ordinary soul.

Eba's attachment was a kind that manifested itself in smiles. The profoundness of his bow was also an excellent gauge of his devotion; had anything happened the day before to jar upon his sensitive nature, his body would be sure to incline itself a little more stiffly than usual. These little congelations would occur when the spray of cherry-blossoms that he had laid on our sitting-room table had remained unnoticed, or when we had declined an offer to take a sunset ride. When all was sailing smoothly on, however, his bow was a thing in which his whole body played a part, and his smile would often degenerate into a grin. I was curious to know something about his home-life ; but my questions elicited no confidences. I often wondered where he stole away in the night-time, and what his own domestic ties might be. But I never learned ; whenever the morning came, there he sat between the shafts of his *jinrikisha*, with the sleepy Cho at his side, and this was the only glance I could get into the manner of his life.

In other more tangible ways, however, did Eba display his kindly spirit. He early learned my admiration for the mountain of Fujiyama, and the desire I felt to view it under the most

promising circumstances. It is not
the easiest thing in the world to see
this capricious peak, owing to the
dense mist that almost constantly en-
velops it; you have to await your
chance, which is not likely to come
many times. Eba took it upon himself to keep a careful watch of affairs,
and spent a large part of his time

with his eyes towards the West. One day he ran into my room in the utmost excitement, and going to the window pulled the curtain aside, with the air of a long-nourished wish fulfilled.

"Come, Mississy, quick," he exclaimed. "See Fuji!"

And there was Fuji indeed, towering in the golden sunset, its outlines clearly marked against the sky, and its summit wrapped in glistening snow.

But his attachment still expressed itself most touchingly in flowers. I know he kept a careful eye upon me to see what I did with his offerings, and when I occasionally wore one of his bouquets, his smiles and bows reached their highest extravagance. One morning he appeared early at the door with a beaming face, though it bore evidence of some anxiety, as if he had formed a plan of the success of which he was doubtful.

"Come, Mississy," he said, pointing to the awaiting *jinrikisha*.

But I was too busy that day, and told him I could not go. He seemed almost ready to cry, and looked up to me again appealingly.

"Some other day, Eba," I returned.

"No, no, — to-day. Cannot see to-morrow."

After a little further conversation, I decided to spend a few moments this way, and so stepped into the *jinrikisha*. He started off in high glee, and ran at a pace that would have terrified me had any other than Eba held the shafts. One or two small children who were so unfortunate as to be in his way were overturned with a single thrust of his arm and went rolling over into the gutter. Eba laughed loudly at his little joke, and shouted

lustily to Cho, who passed us with a
perplexed and disapproving shake of
the head. Finally we drew up before
a florist's shop, and Eba proudly led
the way to the shrine of his peculiar
pilgrimage.

He stopped before a small potted
plant, and pointed at it with a smile.
I was amazed to see a
tiny pine-tree not over
six inches high, but per-
fectly formed in the small-
est detail. I had seen
many other Japanese ex-
periments in minuteness,
but this surpassed them
all. Eba was delighted
with my satisfaction, and
informed me that this
thrifty dwarf had been
growing for many years. It was
to be on exhibition for that day
only, and this explained his anxiety

that I should visit the shop that morning.

When I told my two friends that we were to leave Yokohama, and spend a few weeks in China, their faces suddenly fell, and only brightened when I added that our journey would be a short one, and that we should expect to see them on our return. They carefully inquired when we were to go, and the exact time we were to stay. We thought little of this until, after having spent the allotted number of days in the land of the pig-tail, we rode into the station at Yokohama. During my absence I had given many a thought to the two friends, and wondered whether their thoughts of us had vanished when we ourselves left their sight. I was somewhat surprised, as well as pleased, as the train drew in, to see two familiar figures enjoying the old-time repose between the same *jinrik-isha* shafts. They were Cho and Eba, who eagerly came forward as the train drew to a stop, and scanned the passengers. One or two of those alighting tried to engage their services, but in vain. Eba first caught sight of us, and came up bowing, smilingly followed by the less demonstrative Cho, whose face, however, disclosed that he was a delighted man. Eba later informed us that they had carefully counted the days and the trains, and had hit upon the exact time that we should return.

And now there were more bouquets, more smiles and bows, and more polishing of *jinrikisha* wheels. Again did Eba keep a watchful eye upon Fuji, and many a glimpse of the majestic mountain did I owe to him. But the time came when all this had to end, and when we must sail away from Japan for home. They realised this with regret at least, and during the last few days were more attentive than ever before. Steamer-day came at last, when we should have to bid farewell to our friends, perhaps for-ever. Eba and Cho were not the only ones to regret the parting. They had become such familiar companions, and had served us so faithfully, that we disliked to think that we should see them no more.

Early in the morning of the day of separation I heard a gentle knock at the door. When I opened it I could see nothing at first but a huge bou-quet of beautiful Japanese roses. Presently the roses bowed up and down, and I heard a familiar voice come from behind them. "For Miss-issy." It was Eba's farewell present!

Cho, softened a little at the thought of parting, was also without, and both came into the room and helped us pack our trunks, and performed various little acts of kindness. The ride along the Bund was the slowest we ever took; Eba had lost much of his sprightliness, and Cho's poor old legs lagged more than ever. They insisted on going aboard the boat with us, and tried to find pretext after pretext for remaining, long after their usefulness was over. Finally the last blast of the steam whistle was heard, and Cho and Eba reluctantly moved away.

"Good-bye, Eba! Good-bye, Cho! Perhaps we shall return some day."

"Good-bye, Mississy."

I offered Eba my hand. It was probably the first experience of the kind he had ever had, and he looked at it with a puzzled air. Finally he just touched it with the tips of his copper fingers, and sadly bowed himself away.